NORTH TYNESID

CU00793914

3 8012 00

NORTH TYNESIDE LIBRARIES

<u>LOVE2READ</u>
With our new Love2Read library card
you can borrow 20 books at a time and make unlimited free
reservations all for a £5 annual fee.

Ask for further details on your next visit.

KILLINGWORTH		
1/17	30 JAN 2020	
1 9 MAY 2017	01 NOV 2021	
(R) 2 / 8 / 17		
31 OCT 2017		
- 7 JUN 2018		
1 3 MAR 2019		
- 5 APR 2019		
June 2020		

Please return to any North Tyneside Library by the
last date stamped above or renew online at
www.northtyneside.gov.uk/libraries

follow our story @
www.facebook.com/northtynesidelibraries
http://twitter.com/NorthTyneLibs

SPECIAL MESSAGE TO READERS

This book is published under the auspices of

THE ULVERSCROFT FOUNDATION

(registered charity No. 264873 UK)

Established in 1972 to provide funds for research, diagnosis and treatment of eye diseases. Examples of contributions made are: —

A Children's Assessment Unit at
Moorfield's Hospital, London.

•

Twin operating theatres at the
Western Ophthalmic Hospital, London.

•

A Chair of Ophthalmology at the
Royal Australian College of Ophthalmologists.

•

The Ulverscroft Children's Eye Unit at the
Great Ormond Street Hospital For Sick Children,
London.

You can help further the work of the Foundation by making a donation or leaving a legacy. Every contribution, no matter how small, is received with gratitude. Please write for details to:

THE ULVERSCROFT FOUNDATION,
The Green, Bradgate Road, Anstey,
Leicester LE7 7FU, England.
Telephone: (0116) 236 4325

In Australia write to:
THE ULVERSCROFT FOUNDATION,
c/o The Royal Australian College of
Ophthalmologists,
27, Commonwealth Street, Sydney,
N.S.W. 2010.

THE FACE IN THE MIRROR

The young girl had been standing in the middle of the lane when businessman Edward Graham's car struck her. He took her to a private hospital and said he would pay for her treatment. When she came round, the girl couldn't remember who she was, but she had been wearing a gold bar brooch which spelled out 'Melissa'. No-one came forward to identify her, and Melissa knew she would have to build a new life. But what part would the cold, arrogant Edward Graham play in it?

Books by Sheila Holroyd
in the Linford Romance Library:

ALL FOR LOVE

SHEILA HOLROYD

THE FACE IN THE MIRROR

Complete and Unabridged

LINFORD
Leicester

First published in Great Britain

NORTH TYNESIDE LIBRARIES

BARCODE
00677 8956

CLASS
ROMANCE FICTION

LIB
CUL

LOC
LP

INV DATE
20/1/04

CHECKED
AH

First Linford Edition
published 1999

Copyright © 1998 by Sheila Holroyd
All rights reserved

British Library CIP Data

Holroyd, Sheila
 The face in the mirror.—Large print ed.—
Linford romance library
 1. Love stories
 2. Large type books
 I. Title
 823.9'14 [F]

 ISBN 0–7089–5548–7

Published by
F. A. Thorpe (Publishing) Ltd.
Anstey, Leicestershire

Set by Words & Graphics Ltd.
Anstey, Leicestershire
Printed and bound in Great Britain by
T. J. International Ltd., Padstow, Cornwall

This book is printed on acid-free paper

1

He leaned his dark head back against the leather upholstery of the big car as the chauffeur steered it expertly along the country roads. With eyes closed, he tried to relax, but tension showed in the lines of his firm mouth. His mind was still busy with the problems that the day's meeting had revealed. Plans for the future of that company would have to wait now. Why were people so stupid?

The girl walked steadily along the lane, too deep in thought to be aware of the soft purr of the powerful car's approach behind her until it swung round the curve and its headlights lit up the road. She turned, but instead of seeking safety on the grass verge she seemed frozen, unable to move.

With a hand flung across her face to protect her from the dazzling glare, she stood in the centre of the narrow lane.

The driver had no chance of stopping in time and the car struck her. There was an urgent squeal of tyres as it screamed to a halt, and the two men scrambled out and ran towards the figure that lay like a broken doll on the road's surface. A torch shone on the girl, and lit up her unconscious face.

As the two men kneeled by her, they were unaware that the impact had sent a small case flying into the water-logged ditch. And that the information it could have provided had sunk within minutes under the mud.

* * *

It hurt when she tried to move, and she groaned. There was the sound of quick movement near her.

'I think she's coming round at last,' someone murmured, and when she opened her eyes she saw a pleasant-faced young woman bending over her.

'I don't want to get up yet,' she muttered crossly, and tried to pull the

2

covers over her, but her right arm felt heavy and reluctant to move.

*The woman laughed softly.

'No-one's going to get you up yet,' she responded. 'Just let me lift you a little so you can drink this.'

Her arm supported the girl firmly as she held something cool and refreshing to her lips, and then she watched by the bed until the girl sank back to sleep.

Hours later, the girl woke again. It was still difficult to move, but she was aware that she was lying on a firm bed and that there was an antiseptic smell blending with the perfume of flowers. A small, inarticulate noise escaped her lips. A chair scraped on wood and she heard footsteps approaching her. The woman she had seen before came into view, and this time the girl realised that the white framing her face was a nurse's cap. The soothing voice she remembered came once more.

'Awake again? Now listen, my dear. I'm Nurse Woods. You've had a bit of an accident and you're in hospital.'

The girl's eyes fluttered open wider with alarm and fear, and the nurse hurried to reassure her.

'Don't worry. You're going to be all right.'

'My head aches,' the girl complained huskily.

'I'm not surprised. It got a nasty bang, but this will help.'

Once more the drink was offered her, and this time she managed a faint, 'Thank you.'

'Excellent!' the nurse responded warmly. 'I'm glad you are speaking to us at last.'

When the drink was finished, she wrote carefully on a clip-board which she replaced at the foot of the bed, then drew up a chair and took the girl's limp left hand in her warm grasp, letting the feel of human contact comfort the recumbent figure. She spoke gently and slowly, as if to a child.

'You broke your right arm and leg, so I'm afraid you will have to stay here for a bit. You had no identification on you

4

when you were brought in, so we've labelled your notes Patient X, but we can't go on calling you that. What's your name?'

'My name? I'm called . . . '

The girl stopped and looked at her blankly. Nurse Woods tried again.

'If you tell us who you are, we can get in touch with your family and friends. They'll be worrying about you. Tell us what you are called and we can help you.'

She leaned forward, listening intently, but the girl was silent, frowning, as if trying to solve an unexpected puzzle. Then her good hand desperately gripped the nurse, and she struggled to raise herself on the bed, handicapped by the plaster casts on her arm and leg.

'I don't know!' she said, frightened. 'I can't remember who I am!'

Her eyes filled with panic-stricken tears and Nurse Woods hurried to comfort her.

'Don't worry!' she said reassuringly. 'You've only just woken up properly. I

5

asked you too soon before you'd had time to pull yourself together. Now, time for another sleep, I think.'

This time it was a hypodermic that brought peace, but after the girl lay quiet the nurse stood by her, looking down at the sleeping figure with concern. Judging by the rosy glow that filled the room it was early evening when the girl woke again. She lay still for a while. The room seemed very quiet. She rolled her head very gently and cautiously to the left to inspect her surroundings, and realised that she was in a large, well-furnished room. Thick curtains hung at the tall windows and vases of fresh flowers explained the perfume which had battled with the inescapable hospital smell of antiseptic.

If this was a hospital it was very different from the usual idea of one. She couldn't hear any of the typical sounds of a hospital, such as noises from other patients or the rattle of metal trolleys. The usual medical and nursing requisites might be hidden away somewhere,

6

but it seemed to her more like a room in a luxury hotel.

Then there came the rustle of skirts as Nurse Woods opened the door and bustled in carrying a tray.

'Well done. You're awake just in time for supper, even if it is only soup.'

The girl stared at her.

'I remember. You're Nurse Woods.'

'That's right.'

'I can remember that, but I still can't remember my name!'

The nurse gave her a quick, professional glance, then calmly went on preparing to feed her patient.

'We'll worry about that later. I'll just tuck this napkin round your neck.'

Her hand was pushed away irritably.

'At least tell me where I am and what has happened.'

'I can tell you that while you eat,' and Nurse Woods started to feed the girl spoonfuls of broth.

'Have you ever heard of a man called Edward Graham?' she asked.

'No.' A worried frown appeared

again. 'Should I?'

'He is the man who knocked you down, or rather his chauffeur knocked you down in some country lane when he was driving Mr Graham. He had the sense to call the nearest casualty unit on his mobile phone and get you taken there as quickly as possible.'

The girl gave a wondering look around the room.

'This doesn't look like a casualty unit.'

Nurse Woods gave a gurgle of laughter.

'It certainly isn't! This is Datchett House, a private hospital. The casualty unit found you'd broken your right arm and leg and were badly bruised. Mr Graham had you brought here after they'd treated you. I'm afraid you'll be bed-bound for a while, but your injuries will soon heal, and I can assure you that we'll make you very comfortable here.'

The girl was looking alarmed.

'A private hospital! But this must be very expensive.'

Her hand was patted reassuringly.

'Don't worry. Mr Graham is paying for everything.'

'Why should he?'

The nurse shrugged her shoulders, stacking the bowl and spoon neatly on the tray before wiping her patient's mouth with a linen napkin.

'Remember, he is Edward Graham.'

She saw that this meant nothing.

'Well, he's a man who tries not to attract attention.'

Her patient abandoned this puzzling topic and returned to her main problem.

'I've been trying and trying to remember what I'm called while we've been talking, but everything is a blank before I woke up here.'

'Don't worry. It must have been the shock of the accident. As you get stronger, your memory will come back, you'll see. It may come all at once or perhaps bit by bit. Trying too hard will only get you upset and stop you remembering. Wait till tomorrow. Now, let me settle you down.'

The girl shook her head.

'I don't even know what I look like! Can have a mirror?'

The nurse regarded her doubtfully.

'You're not looking your best at the moment. There are some bruises.'

'Can you think how strange it is not to know what you look like?'

Nurse Woods disappeared for a minute, returning with a hand mirror she had managed to find somewhere and propped the girl up so she could look at herself. The girl's first reaction was a gasp of horror at the deep purple bruises which covered the right side of her face. Then as she looked again she saw big hazel eyes with dark shadows under them, and a generous mouth above a pointed chin. She eyed the mirror carefully, turning her head from side to side.

'Well?' the nurse enquired.

'Well, I'm no oil painting, but it could be worse,' she said with a shaky laugh. Then came a yelp of dismay. 'But what on earth have you done to my hair?'

Her hair touched her shoulders on each side of her face, but on the top of her head it had been roughly chopped almost to the scalp, and irregular bunches stuck straight up.

'You'd had a bang on your head and it was bleeding, so I'm afraid your hair had to be cut so they could treat the wound. Cheer up, it will soon grow again.'

'I hope so!'

She sank down against the supporting pillows.

'So I'm covered in bruises and I've got hair like an old mop, and I still can't remember my name!'

'Don't worry. Wait till tomorrow. There's no rush while Mr Graham is taking care of everything.'

The next morning Nurse Woods came with a doctor who introduced himself as Dr Broadwood. With sure, gentle hands, he made a thorough examination of the girl, and beamed with satisfaction when he had finished.

'As far as I am concerned, my dear, you are making excellent progress. A nice, healthy girl. No evidence of internal injury, Melissa.'

Melissa? She looked at him blankly. The name obviously meant nothing to her, and he sighed gustily.

'Oh, dear, I did hope to jog that missing memory.'

He fumbled in his pocket and finally brought out a small, shiny object which he displayed on his open palm. She peered at it curiously, and then picked it up so she could examine it more closely. It was a gold bar brooch whose twisted metal spelled out the name Melissa.

'You were wearing it when you were knocked down,' Dr Broadwood explained. 'No handbag, ordinary chain-store clothes, nothing in your pockets to give a clue to your identity, just the brooch. We were sure it must be your name.'

It roused no memories. Melissa — an exotic name. She thought of her bruised face and ravaged hair and she shook her head sadly as she gave the brooch back to the doctor.

'I don't feel like a Melissa. It sounds very glamorous, and I'm not glamorous, certainly not at the moment.'

He laughed indulgently.

'You'll feel more glamorous when the bruises have faded. Anyway, the brooch is yours and I will leave it with you. Perhaps the sight of it will have some effect later,' and he laid it on the small table beside her bed.

Left alone, she gazed forlornly at the small, gold brooch, the solitary link with her unknown past, but it struck no chord in her buried memory.

The day fell into a series of snacks and short naps. When she woke in mid-afternoon she became aware of a small sound, the rustle of paper, and realised she was not alone. When she gingerly turned her head on the pillow she saw that a man was sitting in a comfortable chair some distance from the bed, evidently absorbed in writing on a large pad.

Dark hair fell forward over a lightly-tanned face, and she could see high cheek bones and a firm mouth. Some change in her breathing must have alerted him, because he lifted his head, looking at her with cold grey eyes beneath long, dark lashes.

'Do you want the nurse?' he enquired as their eyes met, his voice as cool and detached as his look.

She nodded, and he put his pen and pad down carefully, stood up and strolled forward to stand by the bedside, looking down at her from his considerable height. He was lightly built, elegant in a well-cut grey suit worn with a white shirt and discreet silk tie. Who was he? A doctor? Some hospital administrator?

He pressed a bell-push by her head and continued to look at her as they waited for the nurse to appear. His expression was dispassionate, as though he were looking at an object, not a person. She wondered if this was how he viewed everybody — as inferior creatures with whom he was forced to live.

'Do you know who I am?' he asked.

She shook her head dumbly.

'My name is Edward Graham.'

This produced an effect, though probably not what he had intended.

'You're the man who knocked me down!'

He shook his head in obvious annoyance.

'You stood in front of my car and it hit you.' An impatient note crept into the clear, authoritative voice. 'We couldn't avoid you. You just appeared out of the night in front of the car and made no attempt to move.'

He seemed to expect an apology for her stupidity.

'I'm sorry,' she whispered huskily.

A wry smile touched his mouth briefly as he looked at her bruised face and arm in plaster.

'I suppose you have been punished enough.'

He glanced round the room.

'Is there anything you need?'

'My memory,' she replied bitterly, and then remembered that this man was her benefactor as well as the cause of her injuries, however much she resented his arrogance and obvious lack of real concern.

There was no sympathy in the grey eyes.

'I expect you will recover it in due time,' he remarked, and then the familiar rustle of skirts signalled the arrival of Nurse Woods.

He strolled away from the bed as she entered, nodded briefly to her, and then he left without any further word.

'The arrogance of the man!' Nurse Woods exclaimed as she attended to her patient. 'He takes it for granted he's got visiting rights because he's paying the bills and thinks he can wander in here as he likes to keep an eye on you, and the management lets him! At last you've finally met the famous Mr Graham.'

'Yes, and I didn't even thank him for

16

looking after me!' the girl exclaimed remorsefully.

'I doubt if he noticed.'

'But it must be costing him a lot of money for me to stay here.'

Nurse Woods' lips tightened, indicating no great liking for Mr Graham.

'You don't need to worry about that. I've got a friend who used to work at his house not far from here, so I've heard plenty about him. Oil, ships, construction companies — he's got the lot, and he knows how to spend the money, too. He's not married — now. He was once, but it didn't last. The word is that a lot of women are always eager to comfort him. Still, I wouldn't have him, in spite of his money. A selfish, self-centred type, Mr Graham. So don't you worry about taking what he offers you. After all, it was his car that hit you, and you are going to need all the help you can get!'

She lowered her voice and looked round.

'He probably thinks your accident

17

was just a plan to get money from him and was here checking up on you.'

Her patient brooded on this. She felt mentally as well as physically helpless, aware that all she could do was wait and hope that the doctors could restore her memory as well as her health.

'Why should I do that? It was my fault — at least, I can't remember, but that's what he said.'

The nurse concentrated on straightening the sheets.

'He would, wouldn't he? Let's wait until that memory of yours comes back.'

But it showed no hurry to do so. Most days, Dr Broadwood visited Melissa, as everybody now called her. The bruises faded and she was able to sit up a little, resting against a nest of pillows. Her right leg and arm began to itch under the plaster, and the doctor promised that it would soon be removed. When this was done, she was helped to totter a few steps from the bed to an armchair overlooking the gardens of the hospital.

But even though her body healed, her

memory of who she was refused to return. Her mind seemed to be working normally, but her identity, her past history, seemed to have vanished from her mental record.

'It's so infuriating!' she complained to Nurse Woods. 'I can remember who is Prime Minister and how to wire an electric plug. I can even remember things like the capitals of Europe, but I can't remember my own name!'

Edward Graham appeared again one day with a large bouquet of flowers, and enquired how she felt in a voice which showed no interest in the answer. She embarked on her carefully-rehearsed speech of thanks but he cut her short.

'I could scarcely leave you lying on the road, and I felt it was my responsibility to see you were properly cared for.'

It was a brief visit. They had nothing else to say to each other. Afterwards, she could hear his voice through the half-open door as he spoke sharply to someone.

'You told me her memory would soon return.'

A voice, probably Dr Broadwood's, made some quiet reply.

'But I need to find out who she is!'

Another quiet murmur, then the voices faded into the distance. Melissa strained her ears to hear more, and then sank back with an angry sigh. Edward Graham wanted to know who she was, did he? No sign that he realised how much she herself desperately needed to know! All he cared about was resolving an awkward situation as quickly as possible.

The hospital staff obviously felt it a challenge to help her recall her past. Patiently they showed her pictures of various places, played music, tried to find some interest which might stimulate recollection, but all in vain. Melissa was a well-spoken young woman of approximately twenty-two or twenty-three, and her accent indicated that she came from the south-east of England, but that was all. Her clothes had been of reasonable quality, but all from high street stores. There was no clue there.

Of course, the police had been informed, and a discreet, plain-clothes officer had spent an afternoon with her and asked many questions, but no person had been reported missing who resembled Melissa.

'Anyway,' Nurse Woods commented, 'we know a few things. You probably aren't married.'

She laughed at the expression on Melissa's face.

'You hadn't thought of that, had you? Look.'

She laid her left hand beside the girl's, her fingers spread wide.

'If you wear a ring for any length of time it soon leaves a mark that fades very slowly. I've been married five years, and look at the mark my wedding ring has made.'

She pointed to Melissa's ring finger.

'There's no mark there. You haven't discarded a ring recently, so I doubt if you've left a husband wondering what has happened to you.'

Melissa sat silently frowning.

'No husband, no family enquiring for me. Nobody seems to care about me, do they? Isn't that rather odd?'

The nurse gave her a quick hug.

'I care about you, so don't be silly.'

Melissa gave her a grateful smile, but when the nurse had left she felt sick with worry as she thought of the future. There must be people somewhere who knew her, perhaps loved her. If only she could remember!

Within weeks her body would have healed completely and she would have to leave the hospital. Where could she go? She brooded on her missing identity, fingering the gold Melissa brooch, which was her one link with the missing past. She stared ahead. The past was unknown and the future was just as blank.

2

Melissa sat on a bench in the carefully-tended hospital grounds, but she was unaware of the warmth of the sun and the scent of the full-blown roses. There was a frown on her face, and her attention seemed to be concentrated on the pattern she was drawing with one sandalled foot.

It was five weeks since Edward Graham had followed the ambulance which had carried her unconscious body to hospital. Now her broken limbs had mended, and her face showed no trace of bruises. Only the tufts of short hair on the crown of her head remained as external signs of what she had experienced. The staff of Datchett House had done all that they could for her, and it was time to leave. But her memory had not yet returned, and she did not know where she could go once she left the shelter of the hospital.

She had put off asking the hospital authorities what was likely to happen to her because each morning she woke hoping that her memory had returned and all her problems were solved. She supposed that she would be given into the care of some busy social worker who would find her a room to live, but it was not a prospect she looked forward to. What else could she do, though?

At this point she heard a familiar voice calling from the far side of the hedge.

'Melissa! Where are you?'

It was Nurse Woods searching for her charge.

In the past few weeks nurse and patient had become very friendly. Although it was Edward Graham who had supplied the money, it was Nurse Woods who had bought Melissa the clothes she needed when she was no longer confined to bed. She had made an effort to buy clothes that were becoming as well as practical, and

Melissa had appreciated the trouble she had taken. When Melissa heard her friend's voice she straightened her back and forced a smile to her face. She was very grateful to the nurse for all the care and encouragement she had given her, and she did not want to distress her by revealing how deeply worried she was about her future.

She called back to guide Nurse Woods, who hurried along the path towards her, waving something in her hand.

'A letter for you,' she puffed, sinking down beside Melissa.

'A letter?' The girl's eyes widened in surprise. 'Who would write to me? Who could, when even I don't know who I am?'

Nurse Woods handed her the crisp white envelope.

'Open it and see! I'm as curious as you.'

The envelope was addressed in black ink simply to *Melissa, care of Datchett House*. She opened it slowly, and drew out a single sheet of heavy notepaper. At the bottom of the page the nurse could see the bold black signature of Edward Graham.

'What does he say?' Nurse Woods demanded, shamelessly craning her head to read the letter.

Melissa's eyes travelled slowly down the page.

'He says that he has been told that I am ready to leave hospital now. Since I have nowhere else to go, he suggests that I should spend an indefinite convalescence at his house, Halford Manor.'

She frowned at the brief letter and lifted troubled eyes.

'What shall I say to him?'

'Accept!' the nurse said without hesitation. 'You've nowhere better to go, and it will get you out of this hospital atmosphere. I told you my friend said that it is a beautiful house. Anyway, it is his fault that you're in this situation.'

'If I accept,' the girl said slowly, 'I'll only be putting off the time when I have to learn to cope on my own.'

'You won't be on your own, anyhow. Until your memory comes back you will need people to help you manage. I'm sure I'd prefer luxury with Edward Graham to some bed-sit in a hostel.'

Melissa twisted the letter in her hands. She felt a measure of gratitude for Edward Graham, but when she remembered the coldness of his eyes she realised how much she would miss chatty Nurse Woods and the friendship of the other hospital staff.

'You said that you didn't like him because of what your friend said,' she reminded Nurse Woods.

'I don't expect you'll ever see him. He seems to spend most of his time travelling.'

Melissa looked at the letter again. Halford Manor would give her a breathing space before she had to face the world.

She delayed her reply for a day or two, hoping that her memory would suddenly return and solve the problem, but finally she accepted the offer in a brief note signed simply, Melissa. Events moved swiftly after that.

The hospital administration and Halford Manor organised her being moved. As she waited quietly for other people to arrange her future, it seemed to Melissa that she was caught up in a chain of events over which she had no control. In no time at all, it seemed to her, she was walking out the front door of the hospital carrying a small suitcase.

She had said goodbye to Nurse Woods earlier before she went off duty. The nurse had hugged her and said goodbye with tears in her eyes.

'Keep in touch,' she had urged. 'Let me know how you get on.'

She took Melissa's unresisting hand in her own firm, capable grasp.

'If you need help any time, telephone me. And don't let Edward Graham bully you!'

As she left the hospital, Melissa admitted to herself that she felt a little scared, but this emotion disappeared as she saw the car waiting for her. Her venture into the new world was to start in luxury! Edward Graham had sent a long, sleek limousine to collect her. The driver held the door open for her, and assisted her in carefully.

She sank back in the unaccustomed comfort as the car left the hospital. Looking at the back of the driver's head, she wondered if this was the car which had hit her and whether the chauffeur who was deftly driving the car through the narrow country roads was the man who was driving the car when it hit her. He drove for half an hour through rich farmland, occasionally passing through a small village.

Then the car turned in through wrought-iron gates set in high walls and crawled up a well-kept drive to come to a stop outside a Georgian country house. So this was Halford Manor, her temporary home. The rose-red brick stood with ageless dignity among wide lawns, its simple façade given grace by the careful spacing of generous windows.

Something told Melissa that you often found such houses showing signs of neglect, with empty window frames and flaking paintwork, as the owners fought to maintain their homes in the face of rising costs and dwindling income. But this specimen had obviously benefited from the lavish expenditure of Mr Graham's abundant money. Windows, paintwork, walls gleamed immaculate in the sunshine, and she was sure that no weed could be found in the carefully tended gardens and walks that surrounded it.

As the car drew smoothly to a halt, the distinctive tall figure of Edward Graham himself, dressed casually in beige cotton trousers and a blue shirt, strolled down the flight of steps to meet his guest. When the chauffeur had opened the door and Melissa emerged, his look of calm boredom did not alter as he surveyed her, although this was the first time he had seen her out of a hospital bed.

What he saw was a girl of moderate height, slender after the weeks of illness, dressed in a simple summer skirt and blouse that Nurse Woods had chosen for her. Her pale face had a stubborn line of jaw, and her hazel eyes met his unflinchingly. The hospital hairdresser had done her best, but the uneven length of her hair gave her a faintly urchin look.

When the survey was completed he came forward holding out his hand. His handshake was firm, lasting no longer than politeness required.

'Welcome, Melissa.' His eyes went to the small golden brooch pinned to her blouse. 'I hope it won't be long before we learn your full name.'

Melissa mentally commented, 'Because then I'll be off your hands.'

To Edward Graham, she presented a suitably smiling face and murmured her thanks for his offer of hospitality. Then she was ushered up the steps and into the cool interior of the house. The polished woodwork and the rugs on the chequerboard floor of the hall showed the same care and wealth as the exterior, while great vases of flowers brought the colour and perfume of the garden into the house.

'How lovely!' she exclaimed as she noted the proportions of the graceful staircase.

The owner nodded, as if taking the praise as his due.

'I am very fond of this house,' he remarked, and then turned to a woman dressed in grey who was waiting unobtrusively.

'My housekeeper, Mrs Edgar,' he informed Melissa. 'She will show you to your room. I expect you will want to rest after your journey.'

It had only been a thirty-minute journey, and in fact Melissa was full of curiosity about her new surroundings. She wondered if it was a hint that she was expected to stay tucked away into a room in a corner of this large house for the duration of her visit. But then, as she turned to follow Mrs Edgar, he put out a restraining hand.

'I hope you will be rested enough to join me for dinner tonight,' he said.

Melissa noted a brief look of surprise on Mrs Edgar's face. Obviously this was an unexpected change to the programme.

'Of course, I'll be very pleased to join you,' she responded.

He nodded and turned away, and she then followed the trim figure of the housekeeper upstairs. Mrs Edgar opened a door on the second floor.

'This is your sitting-room,' she said, standing back to let Melissa enter.

It was a large, sunny room decorated in clear, warm pastels with the same attention to unobtrusive, perfect comfort that she had noted on her way through the house. Sunlight flooded in through long windows, and the scent of flowers rose from more vases in the sitting-room and drifted in the window from the flower-beds below. Melissa looked round her with delight, and then Mrs Edgar crossed the room and opened another door.

'Your bedroom and bathroom are through here.'

The same quiet luxury was evident in these apartments as well.

'But this is wonderful! I shall love it here! Thank you for getting it ready for me.'

'I did what Mr Graham asked me to do, and I trust you will find it satisfactory,' Mrs Edgar said in a colourless tone. 'Is there anything you would like now?'

'I'd love a cup of tea,' Melissa said.

'I'll send the maid up with a tray.'

Melissa looked round.

'Perhaps I could have an electric kettle up here so I wouldn't have to trouble anybody in future when I want a drink.'

'I'm sure that could be provided, if you stay here for any length of time.'

There was a touch of feeling in her voice now which made Melissa study her more carefully. The housekeeper was probably in her late thirties, and everything about Mrs Edgar seemed designed to help her avoid attention. Her grey clothes were neat but unflattering, like her mid-brown hair, and her face lacked any animation. When Melissa looked into her eyes, however, she was taken aback by the antagonism she saw there. The next moment Mrs Edgar had broken eye contact and was moving to the door.

'Please inform me if you require anything else,' was her parting remark.

Melissa set about unpacking her few possessions, wondering why Mrs Edgar should dislike her. Perhaps she just objected to the extra trouble of a house guest. After a few minutes there was a discreet knock on the door and a maid came in with a tray of tea things. Melissa poured tea into a fine china cup and sat on the window seat, looking out at a landscaped park. She was glad that Nurse Woods had persuaded her to come to Halford Manor. She might be in limbo, but it was a very pleasant limbo!

Afterwards she explored her small domain. Someone, presumably Mrs Edgar, had provided many little items such as cosmetics and perfumes which a waif would not be expected to possess, and she glanced idly at a selection of books and magazines which had been put ready for her entertainment. Then, mentally tired by the sudden rush of new experiences, she lay down on the white lace coverlet of the bed and fell asleep.

She was awoken a couple of hours later by a tapping on the door. The sun was setting, the room full of its glow as it neared the horizon.

When she called, 'Come in,' the same maid who had brought the tea tray appeared to inform her that dinner would be served in half an hour, and to enquire whether she wanted help in dressing. The offer was politely declined. Melissa showered quickly and put on the dress which Nurse Woods had chosen for any formal occasions, a straight cream crêpe shift which emphasised her slender figure and her hair colour. Then she looked at the array of cosmetics and hesitated, content in the end to use a little eye-shadow and lipstick.

Taking a deep breath, she made her way to the main staircase, reached the first-floor landing, and looked down into the hall. Edward Graham was waiting. He had changed into a light grey suit, and it reinforced her impression of a cold man. As he heard her footsteps on the stairs he turned from the great fireplace where he had been standing and looked up at her.

The last of the sun's rays caught her as she stood at the top of the flight, and he looked up at her without greeting at first, as if admiring a picture. Then he held out his hand and she drifted lightly down towards him, as if beckoned by a magician.

Melissa accepted a sherry in the great drawing-room, its walls hung with pictures against champagne-coloured brocade, but she drank it in silence, wondering what on earth she could say to her host. In the dining-room they sat opposite each other, served by a discreet manservant.

The meal started with cold consommé, refreshing on such a hot day. Then came a white and pink fish dish.

'Sole stuffed with salmon mousse,' Edward Graham informed her as he saw her looking doubtfully at her plate.

She tasted the dish cautiously. It was delicious, very different from the bland fish dishes of the hospital diet, and she ate it with obvious relish.

'I am glad to see you approve of it, anyway,' her host commented.

'It's very enjoyable,' she returned, 'but I don't think I'm accustomed to this standard of food. I suspect I'm really more used to beans on toast. Still, this is good.'

A corner of his mouth twitched as if in amusement at hearing this qualified approval of his cook's efforts. As the meal progressed in near silence, Melissa was aware of her host unobtrusively studying her at intervals. Did he find her pleasant to look at? It was the first time she had worn the dress, and she had been very pleased with the effect when she studied herself in the mirror.

'Wherever you come from,' he remarked finally, breaking a long silence, 'at least you were taught to drink soup and use your fish knife properly. One more clue to your background.'

Her pride in her appearance collapsed abruptly. Melissa scolded herself for her vanity. He had not invited her to dinner so that he could admire her looks, but so he could inspect her table manners! After that comment he made no attempt at conversation, and Melissa began to find the silence oppressive.

She noticed that the cutlery, crockery and glass, although of superb quality, were all very plain in design. The wine goblets were simple, uncut crystal, and the fine china plates were white with a simple silver band.

'Do you deliberately have everything

plain?' she enquired to break the silence.

Edward Graham considered the question and nodded.

'I have found that decoration is often only a disguise for faults. To be simple and beautiful, an object must be flawless.'

'Oh, but . . . ' She found it difficult to express herself tactfully. 'Surely people would not sell you flawed goods.'

She waved a hand at the room and house in general.

'I mean, if you pay for the best, won't you get it, plain or not?'

He laughed cynically.

'You mean money must buy quality? No, I'm afraid not. In fact, I've found that if you are rich some people seem to feel that it is almost their duty to cheat you, to get as much of your money as they can without giving value in return.'

She pondered on this.

'And obviously you mind, apart from wanting quality anyway.'

'Yes,' he replied firmly. 'I work hard

for my money, let others do the same. I will pay what is due, but I will not be seen as a fool to be deceived and robbed.'

His voice had hardened. It sounded almost like a warning.

'How do you know,' she enquired curiously, 'that I am not a fake? Perhaps I haven't lost my memory after all. Perhaps I just wanted to get some of your money.'

He was silent, and suddenly realisation dawned on her.

'That's why I'm here!' she exclaimed, cheeks flaming. 'You can keep me under observation and see whether I've really lost my memory or not.'

She stood up, pushing her chair back hastily.

'I am grateful to you for all you have done for me,' she said, 'but I am not pretending. I'll sign a statement, if you like, saying that I accept responsibility for the accident and want nothing more from you. And I'll pay you back everything you've spent on me!'

41

The manservant had discreetly left the room, and Edward Graham leaned back in his chair and looked up at her, a look of polite attention on his face.

'There is no need for dramatics. If you are genuine, I will help you as best I can. If you are pretending, then eventually I will find out and prove it. Now, shall we finish our meal?'

She sat down, feeling very foolish, and nothing more was said before the meal finished. When they left the dining-room at the end of the meal she hesitated, uncertain what to do next.

'Good-night, Melissa,' he said politely but firmly.

'Oh, good-night, Mr Graham,' she returned, and mounted the stairs to her bedroom.

Here, instead of undressing immediately, she sat for some time staring out over the moonlit gardens. She did not know who she was or how she had survived formerly in the big wide world and Edward Graham was giving her very comfortable shelter for an indefinite time. Yet she did not like Edward Graham, his elegance, his smug self-confidence, or his paranoid belief that everyone wanted his money! But what could she do?

Baffled, she finally undressed and slipped into the nightdress which lay ready and nestled into the welcoming bed.

Downstairs, Edward Graham sipped his coffee and thought about his guest. He had expected a passive female, barely presentable, whom he could virtually ignore. Instead he was giving houseroom to an attractive, spirited woman. Obviously unpractised in hiding her feelings, she had betrayed that she was not particularly impressed by him or his wealth. His wide mouth twitched into a smile of genuine amusement which brought life and youth into his face.

3

Melissa was woken by breakfast being brought to her room, as befitted a recent invalid, and she did appreciate the attention. The last twenty-four hours had been psychologically tiring. Afterwards she enjoyed soaking in a bath scented with an essence chosen at random from the selection available.

Later, she made her way downstairs, wondering what was expected of her. She hesitated in the hall, wondering which door she should open to make contact with other people.

'Good morning.'

She turned, startled by the cool voice, to see Mrs Edgar standing near her. How had she approached so noiselessly?

'Oh! Good morning.'

She hesitated while the housekeeper stood quietly waiting.

'Where's Mr Graham?'

'Mr Graham has left, and will be away for some days on business.'

'He said nothing to me about going away.'

There was a significant silence from the housekeeper, and her look conveyed that her employer was under no compulsion to tell Melissa of his plans. Melissa gestured helplessly.

'It's just that I don't know what I'm supposed to do now I'm here.'

Mrs Edgar looked as if she wondered the same thing, but finally suggested, 'Why not look round the house and grounds today? There's plenty to amuse you, I'm sure. Your meals will be served in your room while Mr Graham is away. Lunch will be at one o'clock.'

It was clear that she felt no obligation to befriend Melissa and was evidently eager to leave her and go about her duties. Melissa thanked her briefly, once again puzzled by the housekeeper's hostility, and made her way out into the grounds. It was the first time since her unknown past that Melissa was alone and free. With no nurse, doctor or host to supervise her, she spent most of the morning roaming in the park. Spring had ended and summer had reached its peak while she was in the hospital, and she enjoyed the warmth of the sun. After lunch in her sitting-room she took a book into a walled flower garden.

In the evening, looking idly into the drawers of a bureau in her room, she found writing-paper and envelopes, and sat looking at their blankness for some time. To whom should she be writing? Who was waiting anxiously to hear from her?

Perhaps nobody, a cold voice whispered. The police had received no enquiries and no-one looking for a girl like her had contacted the various organisations that dealt with missing persons. Perhaps she was completely alone. Friendly Nurse Woods was miles away, and nobody at Halford Manor wanted her there. That night for the first time in weeks she cried herself to sleep with tears of self-pity.

In the morning she reproached herself for her weakness. Look on the positive side, she told herself firmly. You are young, reasonably good-looking, healthy, and being carefully looked after in great luxury. What is there to cry over? Suitably repentant, she set her determined little chin and spent another morning exploring the grounds and the afternoon splashing in the secluded swimming-pool.

The next day the English weather had taken one of its freakish turns, and rain beat dismally against the windows. Bored after some hours of leafing through magazines and watching television, Melissa set out to examine the main rooms of the house, and found herself showing an informed appreciation of the building.

Basically, little had been altered visibly in the two hundred and fifty years since the house was built, but modern conveniences had been installed with the greatest discretion. Decoration, furniture and furnishings

— all were in keeping with what the original inhabitants of the house would have chosen.

The library interested her because of its contents as well as its architecture. Many of the shelves were lined with well-bound copies of commonly-accepted classics, others with books on the history of economics and exploration for mineral resources, but a few shelves bore a very mixed load of modern poetry and novels, obviously the choice of an individual mind. However, she was not sure whether she could take any books from the library to her own rooms, so she concentrated on inspecting the room.

She was standing on some library steps in order to examine the ceiling more closely when she heard the door open. Turning sharply, she tripped and would have fallen to the floor if she had not been caught in the arms that revealed an unexpected steely strength. Edward Graham stood her safely upright and looked down on her from

his superior height with some amusement.

'Does everything meet with your
approval?' he enquired silkily.

She blushed furiously but stood her
ground.

'It is all very impressive, as you must
know. However, I am a bit puzzled by
the plasterwork on this ceiling. It
doesn't seem to go with the rest.'

He gave her a surprised look.

'No. This ceiling was damaged by a
fire in the last century and replastered
then. I know it is Victorian rather than
Georgian, but it's such good workman-
ship that I decided to keep it. I hope you
have noticed that I insisted on the
correct eighteenth-century colours for
decoration, however.'

So he was responsible for the look of
the house and had not left it all to a
hired designer's decision. But now he
wanted answers.

'How did you know it wasn't quite
right?' he asked curiously. 'Very few
people would have realised that.'

She shrugged.

'I just knew. Something out of my past, I suppose.'

He looked at her with measured appraisal.

'That suggests an architectural or art school training,' he commented. 'We must discuss this later at dinner.'

But at dinner no amount of stimulus or direct questioning could find the source of her knowledge. At length she begged him to stop, running her fingers through her hair in desperation.

'I can't remember, I can't! I just get more and more confused instead of anything coming back!'

Obediently he stopped, and for the rest of the meal contented himself with the occasional remark on the weather or the food. This time he suggested that she join him for coffee.

In the drawing-room, when coffee had been served, he said, 'The doctors I have consulted say that it is possible that you can't remember because you don't want to.'

Her eyes widened under the long lashes.

'What a silly idea! Of course I want to remember. It's hateful being in a fog like this.'

'They meant,' he said carefully, 'that your memories might be so unhappy that your subconscious is protecting you by preventing them coming back.'

He watched as she bent her head and considered this. Suppose it was true? Suppose full memory would bring back bitter unhappiness? Then she looked at him and shook her head firmly.

'I don't feel that I am an unhappy or miserable person,' she said slowly. 'I feel like a sensible woman who is probably quite calm most of the time, not the type to make a fuss over nothing.'

'Very possibly true, for most of the time. But suppose something happened, just before the accident, that caused some kind of crisis. You certainly didn't behave like a calm, sensible person when you just stood there and let us hit you. And another thing. Most people

51

are part of a social network — family, friends, job — and that network wants to know what has happened when someone goes missing.

'As far as we can discover, no-one is asking what has happened to you. That suggests that you had somehow dropped out of your circle, possibly deliberately, and that was why you were walking alone along that road in the evening, with no luggage, no means of identity except that brooch.'

He looked at the touch of gold at her throat, the brooch which she always wore. Melissa sighed with frustration.

'What am I to do? I can't go on living here for ever. There must be a limit to how long you'll put up with me.'

She was startled when Edward Graham unexpectedly burst into laughter. She blinked, and indignantly demanded an explanation.

'What's so funny? I think it's just commonsense.'

He stopped laughing, though his expression still showed amusement.

'An attractive woman like you should never think that she might outstay her welcome. She regards her presence as a favour which she bestows on others.'

Melissa was embarrassed by the compliment and bit her lip.

'That may be true of some women,' she said finally, 'but I don't feel attractive,' and her hand rose to touch her uneven hair ruefully.

'But you are,' he said, standing up to indicate the end of the evening as though he had grown tired of the subject and her company. 'I am in no hurry to lose you.'

She was comforted by his statement until later, drifting off to sleep, she suddenly jerked awake. Everything in the house belonged to Edward Graham. Did he now view her as another of his possessions? Attractive women were not like pictures or statues, just to be looked at. They were to be enjoyed by the men who protected them and paid for their comforts.

When Edward Graham offered shelter to the bandaged victim of amnesia it might have been a kind, disinterested gesture. Now that he had a woman he found attractive under his roof, a young woman with no other known attachments, he might expect her to reward him with more than thanks.

If he tried to make advances to her, how would she react? Melissa stared wide-eyed at the invisible ceiling. What would become of her if she rejected him? Would she reject him? She conjured up an image of his tall figure. Many women would find him very attractive, quite apart from his wealth. But she remembered the cold look in his eyes and shivered. She could never respond to a man who saw her only as a toy.

Melissa's late-night speculations seemed irrelevant the next day when she found that Edward Graham had disappeared on yet another business trip. She remembered that she had described herself as calm and sensible, and scolded herself for her overheated imagination. Her novelty made her interesting, that was all.

This time, his absence lasted nearly a fortnight, and she quickly fell into a peaceful routine, finding exercise for her body in the grounds and swimming-pool and amusement for her mind in the library. She found that she appreci-ated and enjoyed the books which the owner of the house had presumably chosen to suit himself. For the first time Melissa felt that they might have something in common.

His return was again as sudden as his departure. She came in from the garden to find the servants bustling about and Edward Graham sitting in the drawing-room with a cool drink. It was a hot day, and his linen suit showed wrinkles from travel, while his frown and the shadows under his eyes indicated exhaustion and bad temper. As she came in he looked up, and she saw the annoyance of a man who was having a much-needed rest interrupted. For a split second he looked at her without recognition.

'You!' he said with a lack of welcome, then shook his head, impatient with himself. 'I'm sorry, I'd forgotten about you. No, that's just as bad . . . '

So much for her fantasies that he might want her! Without being asked, she took his glass and refreshed his drink. He accepted it gratefully.

'I'm sorry,' he repeated, 'but I have been very busy, and I've travelled a long way today.'

'I understand,' she nodded. 'There's no need to apologise.'

They sat in silence while he finished his drink. Then he sighed, put down his glass, and leaned back with his eyes closed. For the first time he looked vulnerable, with signs of strain evident in the lines at the corners of his eyes and mouth. He seemed unaware of her scrutiny, and she realised that he had fallen into a light doze.

Quietly she tiptoed out and closed the door gently behind her. She found herself facing Mrs Edgar, who moved to pass her and enter the room.

'Don't disturb him,' she said, and saw indignant fury flare on the housekeeper's face. 'Mr Graham is asleep,' she explained. 'He is obviously very tired.'

The housekeeper halted, making a visible effort to control herself, and turned away without a word.

Later, the maid brought a request that Melissa join Mr Graham for dinner. This created a minor problem. The few clothes she had brought with her had been selected for an English spring and were proving unsuitable for the warm summer days, and her cream dress needed cleaning. In the end she changed into a long-sleeved cotton blouse and a skirt.

Her host greeted her apologetically.

'My behaviour was unforgivable. First I forgot you and then I fell asleep!'

Obviously he felt he had failed his own high standards of behaviour.

'I'm not surprised you fell asleep. You

57

looked exhausted.'

'I was. The last week has been gruelling.'

He went on to speak of the difficulty of dovetailing complicated plans of action which involved sometimes unreliable partners, of the inflexibility of time and the unpredictability of people. She could not follow all of it, but knew that he was thinking aloud rather than speaking to her. Then he stopped, and seemed really aware of her for the first time that day.

'Thank you for listening so patiently.'

'I'm glad to do something, however small, in return for your hospitality.'

He looked at her with gratitude, and then appreciation.

'It's very rare to find a pretty woman who isn't annoyed when attention isn't centred on her, one who is willing simply to listen to another person's troubles.'

'As I told you before, I don't feel pretty or attractive.'

'As I told you, you are.'

She thought, unconsciously wrinkling her nose.

'When I look in the mirror, I can see I look reasonably good. But I don't feel that how I look is all-important. Well, not as much as what I do or what I'm like. I think I was the kind of person who did something, rather than just existed.'

His eyes still on her face, he enquired, 'Any progress at all with your memory yet?'

Her reply was a doleful shake of the head. Then she brightened a little.

'I think you were right about what I am. I do seem to have a considerable knowledge of buildings. Unfortunately, I can't decide whether I'm an architect, an artist or an estate agent!'

'Well, I haven't seen any newspaper stories about deserted half-built houses or absconding agents!'

They laughed together at the small joke, and finished the meal in companionable silence. Once again coffee was served in the drawing-room, and

Melissa nerved herself to discuss the subject that had started to loom large in her mind in recent days.

'Mr Graham . . . ' she began.

He lifted an eyebrow.

'You have been living here for some time now, and since I can't be equally formal because you haven't got a surname, I feel that you should call me Edward.'

'My missing name is part of the trouble. My memory shows no sign of returning, but I'm perfectly strong now, and I can't go on like this for ever as a permanent guest. Oh, I know that you said I could stay as long as I liked, and you have been very kind in letting me stay. But the truth is that I am getting bored.'

He suddenly choked over his coffee, recovered, and carefully put the cup down, looking at her in disbelief.

'Bored?'

She watched him considering the statement, till he looked at her with open amusement.

60

'My dear Melissa Surname-unknown, do you know how many women have tried to take up permanent residence here in the past years? Dozens have tried on some excuse or the other, and I have had to use drastic methods sometimes to prevent them. You are very definitely the first person to say you are bored here!'

A vivid blush lit her cheeks, and she chose her next words carefully.

'I can understand why people want to live here. It is a beautiful house, and life here is very comfortable. But although I don't know who I am or what I did, I know that I am not used to this kind of life, and I don't want to get used to it.'

Impulsively she thrust her hands forward. They were shapely, but competent-looking and not small.

'I am a worker. I can't just stay here and do nothing, no matter how comfortable life is here.'

He pondered a while, noting how her animation enhanced her looks.

'I can see that to you it is a serious

problem,' he pronounced, 'though it's not one I've met in a woman before. But I know how you feel. I've spent the last few days driving myself to the edge of exhaustion, but the truth is that I know I couldn't stand being idle all the time. You have my sympathy.'

He frowned, concentrating on her dilemma for a while, and then shrugged his shoulders.

'I suppose I assumed that your memory would return one day, that the mental block would clear. If it hasn't done by now, it may never do so.'

She looked at him in horror.

'I said it was a possibility! You could wake up tomorrow and remember everything. Resign yourself to a few more weeks of idle luxury while I see if I can find anyone who may be able to help you medically. If not, we'll have to see about launching you on the world again somehow.'

He looked across at her consideringly.

'You will definitely need help there. Incidentally, are you wearing those unsuitable clothes to dinner because you like them, or haven't you anything better?'

She looked down and glumly fingered the unsuitable skirt.

'I know it's not the most becoming outfit, but Nurse Woods only bought me a few clothes.'

He gave an exasperated sigh.

'Then why didn't you tell Mrs Edgar? She could have got you more.'

'Could I have done? When she said I was to tell her if I wanted anything, I thought she meant small things, like toothpaste.'

'I told her to get you anything you needed.'

She sat silent, biting her lower lip, a mannerism of hers when troubled, while he watched her with lazy curiosity.

'Now what's the matter?'

'I just don't want to become more indebted to you. You paid for the hospital to take care of me, and now you are letting me stay here. I don't want to take too much from you.'

He laughed with real amusement.

'Please believe me. Although you practically threw yourself under my car, I do feel a certain responsibility toward you, and I assure you that I can afford the cost.'

He stopped abruptly, aware that her face had whitened, making her dark eyes seem enormous.

'What's the matter now?'

'I have wondered . . . is that how it seemed to you? Do you think that I was throwing myself under your car deliberately?'

'You mean, were you trying to kill yourself?'

She nodded dumbly. Could something hidden behind the locked door of her memory have driven her to attempt suicide? Was that what she could not remember?

He leaned forward and grasped her hands reassuringly.

'No, you weren't. You were walking along with your back to the car, and when you did hear it you turned round with surprise and stood still. You didn't move toward it.'

She gave a shuddering sigh of relief, and some of the colour returned to her face. They both became aware of his warm grasp on her hands, and he let them go in embarrassment. Quickly he changed the subject.

'It seems to me,' he announced, 'that you should come with me when I next go to London. We can buy you some new clothes, and that should help relieve your boredom. Who knows? A change of surroundings, different activities may bring back that elusive memory. Anyway, all women like new clothes and new people to see them wearing them.'

Her face lit up. She was lonely at Halford Manor when he was away, and a shopping trip to London sounded very attractive. Later, she sat sleepily in front of her dressing-table, brushing her mop of dark hair. When she thought of Edward Graham's generosity and his understanding, her expression softened.

She remembered the comforting touch of his hands. Why had she thought him cold and unfeeling? Then she remembered his cynical parting remark. Why, she wondered, did Edward Graham have such a low opinion of women. Who had taught him to think them vain and self-centred?

4

Melissa woke the next morning with a feeling of excitement and expectation. Her recollection of Edward Graham's plan to take her to London explained why, but she warned herself not to be too helpful. She would probably find that he had already vanished in response to some urgent business call, forgetting all about the suggestion. However, when she came downstairs, Mrs Edgar was waiting.

'I understand from Mr Graham that you are to go with him to London tomorrow,' the housekeeper said. 'Do you need any help before you go?'

'Tomorrow!' Melissa exclaimed in delight. 'No, no thank you. I can manage.'

'Please inform me if you change your mind. Mr Graham seems to be under the impression that I did not make it clear how much I could help you with anything you required.'

There was an undertone of bitterness. Obviously she felt that her employer's rebuke was undeserved. Melissa felt guilty.

'I'm sorry. It wasn't any fault of yours, just my stupidity.'

The older woman bowed her head slightly in acknowledgment of the apology but her manner did not soften.

By the time Edward sent the maid soon after lunch the next day to tell her it was time to leave, she had been ready for some time and she came downstairs clutching the small case with which she had left the hospital. The big, comfortable car was ready to carry them to London. Melissa watched the green fields give way to the suburbs, and then the city itself, and wondered if she had ever made that journey before.

During the journey, Melissa asked Edward Graham where they would be staying, and he told her that he had reserved rooms at a hotel whose name was unknown to her. This disappointed her. Melissa had expected to stay at one of the capital's famous hotels, and had imagined herself in Park Lane, gazing out over London's majestic sky-line. She had forgotten Edward Graham's dislike of publicity.

The car delivered them to an undistinguished entrance in a quiet street, and it was only when Edward had guided her through two sets of doors that the discreet but opulent comfort of the hotel was revealed. This was an establishment that assured its wealthy clients of every luxury, including the luxury of privacy.

A small lift carried them rapidly to their rooms. In the past few weeks Melissa had become accustomed to living well, but as she inspected her temporary home she appreciated the care that had obviously gone into the planning and equipment of the room. The bathroom was a luxurious dream. She laughed aloud with sheer pleasure. What fun it all was!

The telephone rang, interrupting her examination of the toiletries supplied. When she answered, she found that it was Edward Graham.

'I assume you would like an early bedtime after a quiet dinner tonight, so I suggest you order dinner in your room,' he told her.

Her face fell, and her voice made her disappointment clear.

'I'm not tired. You forget I'm not an invalid any more! Can't we go out for a little while, even if it is just to look at the people and the streets?'

Edward Graham had never wandered the streets of a city in his life. He had always been too disciplined, too purposeful for such idle time-wasting. But the girl's urgency reached him. Perhaps for her sake he should try the experiment. She heard him sigh resignedly.

'Very well. We'll go out for half an hour or so. Meet me downstairs in ten minutes.'

As dusk fell, they slipped out of the

hotel and were soon lost in the throng of theatre-goers and sightseers who filled the streets. Everything she saw fascinated Melissa. She gazed at the models in the shop windows. With earthy pleasure she inhaled the smells from restaurants and hot-dog stands. The man with her was far from happy.

He was accustomed to the barrier of space and servants that money and power placed between them and the world in general and felt buffeted by all the people in close proximity, unused to their total disregard of him, their complete unawareness of his identity. Strangers jostled him as if he was of no importance. He felt helpless and vulnerable. He touched Melissa's arm to get her attention, and she turned her glowing face to him.

'If you are feeling tired, we can go back now,' he suggested.

She shook her head, about to deny all trace of weariness, when she saw the tension in his jaw, and realised that he was not sharing her pleasure.

71

'Perhaps I have seen enough for now,' she agreed, and he thankfully led her back to the hotel.

At the entrance, he saw her cast a wistful look backwards at the busy street, and felt a trace of guilt.

'We don't have to end the evening too suddenly,' he remarked, putting a hand under her elbow and steering her toward the lounge. 'We can have a nightcap and watch the other guests. I'll order sandwiches to be sent to your room for later.'

He sank gratefully on to one of the leather couches, a lifted finger bringing a waiter hurrying to take his order. His companion regarded him mischievously.

'You didn't enjoy that one bit!' she announced. 'In fact, I think you hated every second.'

He gratefully swallowed some of his whisky and nodded confirmation.

'I'd never realised before how protected I am from the world. I'm usually in private rooms or offices, and when I do go outside I'm in my car.'

'So, a new experience for you. And for me,' she added with a frown. 'I'm sure I never knew London well. It all seemed strange and exciting, not as if I were revisiting some familiar place.'

'London is big,' he returned. 'It's more like several small towns or villages than one big city. Tomorrow we may visit some place which you'll recognise. In view of your interest in architecture, we might try the Victoria and Albert Museum.'

'Museums?'

He smiled with a touch of malice.

'Very educational. We could try the Science Museum, the Natural History Museum, and the Geology Museum. You'll love them!'

Before she could respond to his teasing they heard a cry of, 'Edward! Edward Graham!'

They looked up and saw a well-groomed man in early middle-age bearing down on them. The stranger shook Edward's hand warmly.

'Glad to see you! I heard about your

dealings in Hamburg and wanted to . . . '

His voice died away with the sentence unfinished. He had seen Melissa. She gave him a friendly smile, unaware of the way it intensified her fresh charm.

'Melissa, let me introduce Gordon Cardus,' Edward said resignedly. 'He may look like an over-age rugby player, but he's actually a very astute merchant banker.'

'Pleased to meet you,' Cardus said, eagerly shaking her hand. 'What a delightful name! Is your surname just as suitable?'

'Just call her Melissa,' Edward instructed him. 'It's what I do.'

'Oh.'

Cardus looked from Melissa to Edward and then back again. It was obvious that he was leaping to some very wrong conclusions.

'Well, Melissa, Edward, I didn't mean to intrude,' he said with heavy tact, 'so I'll leave you now. Perhaps I can call you tomorrow, Edward, and

74

make an appointment.'

'For goodness' sake, sit down, Gordon,' Edward said with amusement. 'You've got it wrong. Melissa is living with me.'

'Then I haven't got it wrong,' Gordon Cardus said, still poised for departure.

'Yes, you have. Sit down, man, and have a drink while I explain,' and the waiter was summoned again.

Gordon sat warily on the edge of his seat as Edward began his explanation of Melissa's presence and why she lacked a surname. By the time he had finished, Gordon had relaxed and was patting her hand with paternal sympathy.

'You poor girl! Of course, Edward is right. We'll have to take you all over the place till we can jog your memory.'

Edward noted drily that Gordon had joined the list of memory-joggers without invitation, but resigned himself to the fact that the main aim of the visit to London was to help Melissa, after all. His own memory stirred. Perhaps Gordon had one special advantage.

'Is your wife still as devoted to shopping?' he asked.

Gordon laughed.

'Of course! It's her hobby, and a very expensive one. She could write a very good guide to the dress shops of London. After all, she knows more about them than any other woman!'

'Then perhaps she can help us. One of the reasons we came to London was to fit Melissa out with some new clothes. Perhaps your wife could help her — take her to the right shops, tell her what's in fashion. I would be most grateful for her help,' he said with some meaning.

Gordon Cardus sat back.

'You mean, you'd like Carole to take Melissa shopping for a complete wardrobe? Go round London buying clothes? She'll be delighted to help!'

'Are you sure? I don't want to put her to any trouble,' Melissa said gratefully.

'I'm quite sure,' he responded firmly.

Even if his wife had not been such a dedicated shopper, he would have

76

insisted that she help. Any chance to put the influential Edward Graham under any obligation, however slight, could not be missed.

'Caroline will be in contact with you early tomorrow,' he assured Melissa.

'Do you think she could help me to get my hair cut properly as well? I'm tired of looking like a mop!'

Gordon smiled at her triumphantly.

'I forgot to tell you that she knows nearly as much about beauty salons as she does about dress shops!'

Finally he took his leave, and Melissa sank back in her chair. Edward looked at her just in time to see her try to stifle an enormous yawn. She gave him a sleepy grin.

'I think the journey and the first sight of London have tired me after my quiet country existence,' she admitted. 'Perhaps it's time I had those sandwiches and went to bed now. Tomorrow is going to be a full day!'

Meanwhile, Gordon Cardus got home to find his wife preparing for bed, brushing her thick, dark hair. A tall woman with a striking figure and long legs, she gave her husband a look of affectionate suspicion.

'You have a certain look about you,' she said. 'What are you up to?'

'Nothing!' he protested. 'At least, nothing you can object to. Can you cancel any arrangements you've made for tomorrow? I want you to do me a little favour.'

When he had explained what the little favour was, Carole Cardus sat silent for a while.

'Correct me if I've got it wrong,' she said, 'but you want me to spend a day taking a young woman round the shops of London to buy her clothes. Money is no object, and you say I can buy myself a present as well?'

'Remember, you've got to get her hair done as well,' her husband said. 'That really does need attention.'

A blissful smile spread across his wife's face, and her dark eyes glowed.

'It sounds like heaven!' she said. 'Of

course I'll do it.'

'Good. And I think you'll like Melissa.'

Carole looked at him consideringly.

'Do you believe what Edward Graham said about her, that he's just looking after her till she recovers her memory? Are you sure they're not lovers?'

Gordon shook his head decisively.

'Graham wouldn't lie. He's too arrogant to care what people think. Anyway, wait till you see Melissa. She's attractive, but not the sophisticated type he goes for.'

'That might be why he likes her,' his wife said enigmatically.

Only Carole Cardus knew how she persuaded a very fashionable hairdresser to find time to attend to Melissa's hair early the next morning, but at nine o'clock Mrs Cardus arrived at the hotel by taxi and swept into the reception area where Melissa and Edward Graham were already waiting. Melissa felt overwhelmed at the sight of the strikingly elegant figure in the perfectly-fitting black suit, but Carole smiled brilliantly at Melissa as Edward introduced her as Mrs Cardus.

'If we are going to spend the day shopping together, we can't be formal,' she stated, 'so you must call me Carole.'

Rapidly she cast an appraising eye over Melissa's slender figure. There would be no problem in buying clothes for this girl. She was going to enjoy the day!

'I gather Gordon has explained what is wanted,' Edward said quietly to Carole as he ushered the two women to the taxi which Carole had instructed to wait for her. 'Get Melissa whatever you think is necessary, and either have the bills sent to me or tell me later how much I owe you.'

He smiled meaningfully at her.

'Of course, I hope you will include something for yourself to compensate you for your trouble.'

Carole smiled sweetly back at him.

'I'd better warn you that I'm going to take an awful lot of trouble.'

They looked at one another in perfect mutual understanding.

The first call was at the salon, where the hairdresser turned pale at the sight of Melissa's butchered locks and then set to work to reshape them. She protested when he began to cut the rest of her hair short.

'I can't imagine myself with short hair! I'm sure it has always been at least shoulder-length.'

'Quantity alone is not always best. The shape is all-important,' he said and indeed the short, feathery style which he created brought out the elfin delicacy of Melissa's features which the longer hair had tended to obscure.

While the hairdresser worked, Carole Cardus was busy listing what she considered essential purchases.

'I thought we should go straight to Knightsbridge to start clothes shopping,' she informed Melissa, who frowned in surprise.

'I thought all the big chain stores were in Oxford Street,' she commented. 'Wouldn't it be easiest just to work along there?'

Carole was struck dumb. She gave an agonised look at the hairdresser, who came smoothly to her support.

'But Mrs Cardus is famous for her taste! You must let her show you the best that London has to offer.'

And that was just what Carole did. By mid-afternoon, with a brief pause for lunch, they had tracked down many items, and broke off for afternoon tea and a chance to consider what they had acquired and what remained to be obtained. Heads together, they ticked and compared lists in perfect harmony. There had been minor hiccups. At most places money had not been mentioned, but once Melissa had accidentally seen the price of a particular dress, and was so shocked that she had almost refused to buy it. It had taken all Carole's powers of persuasion to convince her that Edward would consider it very reasonable, if he thought about price at all.

Now she put her cup down and added a squiggle to the list.

'I know a shop which has some wonderful lingerie,' she declared. 'We must go there next. We can stop at the other shops on the way.'

Then she looked at Melissa mischievously.

'I must say, dear, that I am thoroughly enjoying myself, spending money like this without having to think what Gordon will say. But I would like a little reward for my effort.'

'I thought the beaded silk jacket was your reward,' Melissa retorted, now completely at ease with the other woman.

'Don't tease me! That's my reward from Edward, but I would like something from you, too.'

She lowered her voice confidentially and leaned nearer.

'Satisfy my curiosity. Tell me the truth about you and Edward.'

Melissa gave an undignified gurgle of laughter.

'I thought Gordon had told you about me and Edward.'

'Oh, he told me some story about you losing your memory and Edward rescuing you. Don't tell me that's the truth.'

Melissa nodded solemnly, but her eyes were still laughing.

'I'm afraid so. I lost my memory after Edward's car knocked me down so Edward seems to see me as his responsibility, a lame duck to be helped, and so far I haven't been able to come up with any alternative.'

The older woman looked at her sceptically.

'Do you want to? It seems to me that any woman who is lucky enough to have Edward Graham looking after her is not likely to be in a hurry to find an alternative.'

'That's what he seems to feel. But I feel so helpless and dependent, and I don't like it. Sometimes I feel I'm in a very comfortable prison.'

'A lot of other women would like to be in that prison,' Carole stated.

Melissa turned to her.

'Now it's your turn. Tell me about Edward, because I know very little about him really. Somebody told me that he has escorted some beautiful women, though I haven't seen any sign of them. I suppose he won't bring any to Halford Manor while I'm there.'

Mrs Cardus crossed her slim legs and sat back. Gossip was her second favourite activity, after shopping.

'I can only tell you what I've heard, which is mostly rumour. Gordon has had quite a lot to do with him in business matters, but Edward has always kept his personal life private.'

She waited while their cups were refilled.

'I know he took over control of affairs quite young, when his father died, and he is an excellent businessman, far richer now than when he inherited. But he doesn't seem to have much fun with his money really. Obviously, he is very eligible, and a lot of women would like to catch him. He knows this, of course, and he certainly hasn't rejected them all.

'However, there's been very little gossip. The relationships have been very discreet, and never seem to last more than a few months. I did meet one girl who told me that he was very generous and very considerate, but she never felt that he really cared about her. So she left him for a man with half his money who adored her. Mind you,' she added honestly, 'half Edward's money is still a very nice amount.'

'But he was married once,' Melissa ventured.

Carole's face clouded and she stirred her cooling tea.

'You mean Leonie. That was about ten years ago. She seemed the perfect wife for him. She was well-bred, used to the kind of society he lived in, and very beautiful. I met them together a few times. They said and did all the right things, but there never seemed to be any warmth between them.

'Leonie expected constant attention and admiration, and I think Edward was too busy to provide them, and perhaps he didn't care enough to make the effort. We were all surprised when she left him after two years for a rich Greek. She married him after Edward divorced her. Sadly, she died a couple of years ago in the South of France. Well, Edward returned to his bachelor ways and hasn't shown any sign of trying marriage again, so you can see why I thought you might be his latest girlfriend, though I admit none of them has ever needed help in spending money.'

A small frown creased Melissa's forehead.

'Poor Edward,' she said softly.

Carole looked at her sharply.

'Don't start feeling sorry for him,' she said. 'He's got money, power and intelligence. If he's not satisfied with his life, he can change it.'

'Money and power can't make people love you. They just make you doubt whether people can really like you for yourself. I think his coldness may be a defence to protect a very lonely man.'

'Don't say I didn't warn you! You sound too soft-hearted, Melissa. You're a lot more vulnerable than he is. Whoever you are, you're an innocent compared to our Mr Graham.'

She looked at Melissa's face, and saw how little effect her words had had.

'Look, I don't know what's going to happen to you, but if you ever get into a situation where you need help, then you can call me.'

She handed Melissa a little card.

'That gives our home number, so keep it safe.'

Then she rose purposefully.

'Come on, we need a taxi.'

It was in the next shop that Melissa fell in love with a dress. It was beautiful, but the price was extortionate. Even Carole Cardus hesitated when she learned how much it cost, but Melissa tried it on, and was lost. She stroked its soft folds with awe. It was without doubt the most beautiful dress she had ever seen. She took a deep breath.

'I'll take it,' she said defiantly.

At the end of the day, the two women parted firm friends, and when Edward Graham, back at the hotel, asked politely how the day had gone, he was almost overwhelmed by Melissa's enthusiastic account of the day.

'I was very extravagant over one dress, though,' she said guiltily.

'Wait till I see the dress. Then I'll tell you whether it's worth it. Incidentally, I thoroughly approve of the hairstyle.'

At the door to her suite, Melissa turned to Edward. In spite of her fatigue, her eyes were shining.

'I've had a lovely day, Edward. Mrs Cardus was wonderful, but you made it possible. Thank you.'

Then she was gone, leaving him oddly touched. It was not often that his wealth produced such simple gratitude.

5

While Melissa had been shopping, Edward Graham's business contacts had been clamouring for his attention. He had been intending to escort Melissa round London but the next day rapidly became filled with unavoidable meetings.

'I'm not sure what you can do,' he said when they met in the morning. 'Would you like to stay in the hotel and rest, or would you like the chauffeur to take you somewhere?'

Melissa thought back to that first evening in London, and the short walkabout that she had enjoyed so much.

'I'd like to explore, all by myself. I want to go to Piccadilly Circus, then find Bond Street and all the other places I've heard of. I can manage.'

'Are you sure?'

The determined chin jutted forward, and she gave him a militant glare.

'Just give me a chance to show you!'

'Oh, well, you can always get a taxi back if you want you. Speaking of taxis, have you any money?'

This was something that had not occurred to her, and she shook her head slowly.

'Not a penny!'

He took out his wallet, extracted some notes and gave them to her.

'Enjoy yourself, and come back safely.'

She took the money rather reluctantly. Of course she knew that even without the clothes she had bought the previous day Edward Graham was spending money on her, but somehow there was a difference between accepting free accommodation and taking hard cash from him.

Then one of the hotel clerks approached to murmur discreetly that a car was waiting for Mr Graham, and he turned away, forgetting Melissa as he prepared to deal with business matters.

She was surprised how uncertain she felt and how her heart thumped as she left the hotel clutching a map of Central London supplied by a receptionist. Then she told herself that it was only to be expected. After all, it was the first time for months that she had gone anywhere unescorted, and this was a strange city to her as far as she knew.

When her initial nervousness had passed she spent an enjoyable couple of hours wandering round some of the famous landmarks. She ate lunch in the restaurant of a large public art gallery, and then resumed her sightseeing. She felt free and happy, part of the crowds. No-one here knew that there was anything odd about her, that her memory went back only a few weeks.

By mid-afternoon, her mood was changing, however, as she grew tired. Everybody around her appeared to be in couples and families who formed happy supportive groups, but she was alone. No-one looked at her with recognition or even acknowledgement of her existence. Only one person felt any responsibility for her. She lifted her hand and hailed a taxi back to the hotel where she waited for Edward Graham.

When he returned to the hotel he found her having tea in the lounge. She looked composed, but a little pale.

'Did you enjoy exploring London?' he enquired.

'Very much, though I'm afraid it didn't jog my memory.'

He sat down opposite her while she chatted about the sights she had seen and what she had done. Then she fell silent, and Edward looked at her intently.

'Are you tired?'

She nodded, and gave an exasperated laugh.

'It's annoying to have to admit it, but perhaps I tried to do too much, and although I've enjoyed my day of liberty, perhaps two non-stop days have over-taxed my strength. I'll be pleased to get home.'

Edward's heart gave an unexpected lift when he heard her talk of going 'home' and realised that she meant back to the country, to his home. This surprised him. He was usually reluctant to share Halford Manor with others, but when the chauffeur brought the big car back to the hotel the next morning and Edward helped Melissa to her seat, he was glad that she was returning with him. On her side, she felt a new companionship with him, and felt that what she had learned about him from Carole gave her more insight into his complex nature.

The venture to London had not restored her memory, but there was a fast-growing bond of friendship and respect between them. All the excitement was not over, however. They had brought many of Melissa's purchases back with them, but some things had needed slight alterations, and deliveries continued to arrive for some days.

The beautiful dress which she had bought on impulse had been one of the garments which needed minor adjustments and proved to be the last thing to arrive. She found it waiting for her late one afternoon when she came back from swimming and she carried the grey and gold box into her bedroom where she opened it carefully and one by one lifted out the many layers of tissue paper until finally the dress itself was revealed.

She touched it with gentle fingertips, and then took it out and spread the skirt wide on the bed. It demanded to be worn, and hastily she took off her summer dress and slipped the gown over her head. Then she opened her eyes and looked in the mirror. It was as beautiful as she had remembered. The dress was a drifting haze of blue-green silk chiffon, the fabric so light that it floated in the slightest current of air. She was taken aback by the picture she made.

The dress flattered and enhanced her slenderness and intensified the clear pallor of her skin, while her dark eyes seemed to have grown even larger. She twisted and turned, looking at herself from every angle in the full-length mirror. But her own admiration was insufficient. The dress needed an audience.

Just then the gong sounded for dinner. She had lost track of the time. Edward Graham would be waiting for her. She would have to change, and what could she wear? Then she looked in the mirror again. Why should she change? With growing excitement, she swiftly applied some lipstick and mascara.

Edward Graham, waiting for her in the hall, looked up to see enchantment drifting slowly down the staircase. He stood silent, unmoving, as she descended and came towards him. She stopped a few feet from him, puzzled by his lack of reaction.

'Don't you like it?' she said hesitantly. 'I know it's not really suitable for a quiet dinner at home, but I couldn't resist wearing it.'

Still he was silent, and she turned,

head drooping a little, to go back up the stairs.

'I'll change it,' she said despondently.

He seemed to wake up suddenly, like a man coming out of a dream, and approached her with hands outstretched.

'No,' he said, his voice barely under control. 'I just couldn't find words. Thank you for showing me such a beautiful dress on such a beautiful woman.'

Her mood changed immediately, a flashing smile replacing the look of disappointment. This was the proper reaction to the dress, she felt. She took his hand and bobbed an impromptu curtsey. Then they went in to dinner.

Throughout the meal, he was even quieter than usual, but Melissa hardly noticed as she talked happily about their visit to London until she looked up and found his look fixed on her. She wondered what he was thinking behind those grey eyes.

In fact, he would have had difficulty

in telling her. His logical brain was finding it hard to cope with his mixture of emotions. Long accustomed to lovely women who tried to charm him, he had observed and admired Melissa's fresh good looks objectively, without any emotional response, regarding her as a temporary and amusing dependant who made few claims on him.

The time in London had shown him how other men like Gordon Cardus would react to her, but he had found himself more aware of her open personality and warmth, touched by her apparent fresh response to so much that he took for granted. He had seen that she was attractive to others, but had felt himself immune. Now, however, when he had not been expecting it, the recent invalid had turned into a beautiful charmer.

The primitive masculine ego asserted itself. She was under his roof, fed and clothed by him, and he wanted her. But she was his responsibility and she trusted him to look after her and protect her. He could not let himself take advantage of his position.

Dominated still by years of caution and rigid self-control, he made an excuse to leave her as soon as the meal ended, leaving her to wonder at his terseness. Melissa was disappointed by the way he seemed to ignore the impression she made in the dress after that first reaction. Left to her own devices, she sat in the drawing-room and leafed through a magazine, but it could not interest her. The dress demanded more than sitting alone till bedtime. It deserved to be seen in movement, at a ball.

She stood up and started to hum a waltz. Slowly she lifted her arms and began to glide over the polished, wooden floor. She sang on, twisting and turning as though dancing with some invisible partner. Her hair lifted in the rhythm of the dance, framing her rapt face. In the dimly-lit room she could see her figure faintly reflected in the huge wall-mirrors.

Suddenly she was aware of Edward silhouetted in the open door. How long had he been watching her? But she did not care and danced on, gradually sweeping closer to him until he took the inevitable step forward and his arms went round her and the dance continued. But this was no dream partner. He drew her closer and closer, until their feet stopped and her song fell silent. Still they stood locked together, and she lifted her face to his, her body soft and compliant in his arms.

His kiss, his embrace, was urgent and demanding.

★ ★ ★

Melissa's breakfast was pushed aside, hardly touched, as she dressed hurriedly, eager to see Edward again. She checked her appearance before she left her bedroom. Happiness was making her hazel eyes shine and her skin glow. For once, she thought, she did indeed look beautiful.

She skipped downstairs, half-expecting him to be waiting for her at the bottom as he had done yesterday evening, but the hall was empty, and no door was flung open to greet her. She checked a moment, and then decided to go into the drawing-room. Edward Graham was there by the great windows, gazing out over the gardens, and he did not turn, even though he must have heard her come in.

'Edward,' she said hesitantly.

He turned then, hands in pockets, and stood there, making no move to come to her. His face was as cold, set and stern as when she had first seen him all those weeks ago. The brightness faded from her face.

'What's the matter?' she faltered uncomfortably.

He turned his head away as if he could not bear to look at her.

'Last night, what I did was wrong. You are a sick woman, Melissa, and I should not have taken advantage of you. I apologise. It will never happen again, and if I can do anything to compensate for my behaviour . . . '

She was motionless for only a moment, and then, before he could guess what she intended, she strode forward and slapped him, hard. His hand instinctively went up to his face, and then shock was followed by fury, but she stood before him with hands clenched and cheeks red with anger that equalled his own.

'You idiot! You conceited, arrogant, insulting fool! I've lost my memory, but that's all that's wrong with me! I'm not sick! How dare you say that you took advantage of me? Do you think I'm so stupid that I didn't know what effect the dress and the dance and the moonlight were having? If anything, I seduced you.'

The red mark of her hand stood out on his white cheek.

'But you are under my protection!'

'And who was to protect you from me?' she said challengingly.

They confronted each other, eye to

eye. Gradually the anger faded. A younger, tentative Edward could be seen.

'You mean you really wanted me?'

She sighed, and putting up her hand she tenderly stroked the red mark.

'Didn't I make that clear last night?'

He caught her hand by the wrist and turned his head so that he could kiss the captive palm.

'I wish with all my heart that I could believe that!'

She tilted her serious, intent face and gazed into his troubled eyes.

'I don't lie, Edward. You can believe it. Let me prove it.'

And she drew his head down to hers. When they finally drew apart she looked at him reproachfully.

'Admit you were a fool.'

He gave her an uncertain smile.

'I hope I was. Yes, I was! I'm sorry.'

She sighed, and then laughed a little breathlessly.

'And I apologise for hitting you. But after I'd raced downstairs expecting to be greeted by your open arms, to be told instead that it would never happen again did provoke some strong feelings!'

'If I ever rouse similar emotions in you again, I'll take care to stay out of reach!'

They laughed together, and Melissa looked at him with satisfaction.

'If nothing else, I've seen you smile and I've made you laugh. I don't think you've had enough simple happiness in your life. How do you feel now?'

He tightened his arms round her.

'Happy, and hungry. I couldn't eat this morning, wondering how I could face you.'

'Then let's call Mrs Edgar and have breakfast together, for the first time.'

It was an enchanted day. They wandered happily together in the sunfilled gardens, with little to say but content to have the other near. Sitting in a garden where the crimson blaze of the roses was joined by the trickle of water from a small fountain, Edward lovingly observed the clear line of Melissa's profile as she closed her eyes and lifted her face to the sun.

'I've never known anyone before who could get such pleasure from little things,' he observed. 'You enjoy something so whole-heartedly — the sun on your face, the crowds in London . . .'

'Don't forget baked beans,' she reminded him laughingly.

'No! I must tell the cook to make sure we always have some in stock.'

She didn't reply, and he glanced down to see that her face had grown suddenly serious.

'Always?' she echoed.

He nodded, still watching her.

'If it sounds like a commitment, that's what I meant it to be as far as I'm concerned. I love you, Melissa, so I want to be with you always.'

She bit her lip thoughtfully, remembering what Carole had told her, and looked at him with a troubled expression.

'Are you sure? You don't have to make any promises to me. After all, you have power and money, which gives you choice. In time you'll get used to me, and perhaps start to wonder about all the other choices you could have made. I'll take the love you can give me while you can.'

He shook his head decisively.

'I've made choices in the past, and regretted them. I won't regret choosing you. Do you think you'll be sorry?'

Her eyes looked back at him steadily.

'Never. Whoever I've been and wherever I've been, with you I feel I've come home.'

They held each other without speaking, then he gently released her and sat back, holding her hands.

'We might as well get the formalities over, Melissa, and I can't imagine a better time or place. Will you marry me?'

She looked at him in complete surprise, her eyes growing larger.

'Marry you?' she said with disbelief.

He nodded firmly.

'Please say yes. I want everyone to

know that we will always be together.'

Troubled, she bent her head to avoid his gaze.

'But you have been married before. Didn't you think that would be for ever?'

His head jerked up sharply before he frowned.

'I suppose Carole Cardus told you. I would have told you myself in time.'

Bitterness crept into his voice.

'I was young, but I was already managing a business empire, and managing it well. I used to spend the day surrounded by people who saw me as the most important man in the world. Then I used to go home to an empty house and loneliness. So, I decided I needed a wife and family. There were plenty of eligible women but then one evening I met Leonie, and she was the most beautiful woman I had ever seen. In fact, I don't think I've ever seen her equal.

'Of course, being young and inexperienced I confused lust with love and asked her to marry me. It was only after we were married that I realised that I was unimportant to her. It was my money she wanted. I found that she was cold and selfish. Her beauty and her vanity were all-important to her, and she demanded constant admiration, but even then the marriage might have survived if she had been willing to give me the family I wanted. But children were out of the question. They might have spoiled her beautiful figure. After that discovery, it was just a matter of time before we broke up.'

Melissa watched him with silent sympathy, seeing how that old rejection by his wife had hurt him.

'After that, it seemed safer not to take the risk of making another mistake, so I settled for relationships where there were no promises, no commitments.'

Melissa leaned forward and kissed him gently on the lips.

'But I promise you,' she said softly, 'that I will never leave you while you want me to stay, because I love you, and

I commit myself to you for as long as we love each other.'

'Then will you marry me?'

She took a deep breath.

'Marry you? Oh, yes, Edward.'

But even as his face lit up she stopped abruptly, and gave a cry of despair.

'What's the matter?'

She had suddenly remembered the obstacle between them.

'How can I marry you when I don't know whether I'm already married or not!'

He sank down beside her, appalled. Her missing memory had made so little difference to their relationship that he had forgotten that problems from her past life might affect them now.

'Listen!' he said at last. 'Do you feel you might stop loving me if your memory came back?'

She thought for a while.

'No, I don't think so. I can't imagine that anything in my past could over-come this new emotion, this love for you. But how can I say for sure until I know who I am and what I have been?'

He held her fiercely, as if defying fate to part them.

'Then we will marry. Somehow we'll cure your amnesia, and then we'll marry, whatever is revealed. I promise you that we shall be together for always, my dear Melissa.'

6

Once again Melissa's life had been transformed. Instead of being a house guest, she had become the adored centre of Edward Graham's life. He was a different man. The defensive shell which had shown itself as arrogance and coldness had vanished before her generous love and in the time they could spend together they both knew perfect happiness.

The rest of the world could not be ignored, however. One morning Melissa suggested that they have a picnic lunch in the garden. When Edward agreed, she asked Mrs Edgar to supply suitable food. Later, as she was crossing the hall, Melissa heard the housekeeper's voice coming from the drawing-room.

'The young lady has asked me to prepare a picnic for the two of you, sir. Is that what you want?'

Edward's reply was short but positive.

'Do as she asks. In future, if Melissa wants any changes in what we have for our meals, or in anything to do with how the house is run, then her wishes are to be obeyed.'

There was a brief pause, and then Mrs Edgar's voice protesting.

'But, Mr Graham, I am the housekeeper. I thought you were satisfied with my work.'

'I was, Mrs Edgar, but from now on it is Melissa's wishes that count. You will do anything that she asks you to do, just as you would follow my own instructions.'

There was no reply, just the sound of footsteps, and Melissa saw Mrs Edgar come out of the drawing-room, stony-faced.

News of Melissa's altered status spread rapidly. Servants who saw her as possibly their future mistress became eager to please, occasionally over-eager. She could not help seeing, however, that their eyes held speculation and a touch of contempt. Melissa realised that to them she was a woman who had used her youth and proximity to trap a rich and lonely man. Because nothing was said, she could do nothing to defend herself.

Edward continued his policy of not allowing work to intrude on his home, and Melissa had to resign herself to frequent absences. Then he had to go to Holland for a week and Melissa missed him sorely, in spite of the frequent telephone calls.

She welcomed him gladly when he returned. She only felt whole when he was with her, as though they were the two parts of one being. His embrace told her that he felt the same.

'Let's go to the rose garden,' he suggested soon after his return, and when they were sitting on the bench where he had asked her to marry him, he produced a small box from an inner pocket.

'I had to bring you a present,' he said lovingly as he opened it.

It was a ring, one large, beautiful diamond centred between six smaller stones. She gazed at it wordlessly.

'We may not be able to marry yet, but that doesn't stop me giving you an engagement ring,' Edward said.

He took her left hand and slipped the glittering diamonds on her ring finger.

'Do you like it?'

She nodded, eyes fixed on the shimmer and the dazzle of the jewels.

'I guessed the size pretty correctly,' he said, his lean fingers adjusting the ring. 'It's a little big, however, so be careful of it.'

'I don't think I dare wear it! It must have cost you a fortune.'

He shrugged.

'Think of it as a lump of carbon, a glorified version of coal, and you won't be so worried,' he said carelessly. 'The important thing is that it signifies to everyone that we love each other and intend to marry.'

To us, perhaps, she thought, but other people will see it only as a sign of how I can get valuable presents from you.

'I shall keep this ring as a symbol of what we mean to each other, and because I think it's beautiful, but you mustn't think that you have to give me extravagant gifts,' she protested.

'You give me more. I feel as if I've been existing, not living, for the past ten years, but you are bringing me back to life.'

She forgot her worries about the ring until she saw Mrs Edgar eyeing it some hours later. Tired of the silent antagonism, Melissa decided to challenge it. Impulsively she thrust out her hand.

'Do you like it, Mrs Edgar?'

The housekeeper inspected it impassively, then commented coldly, 'It's a beautiful ring. I am sure you won't think the price too high to pay.'

Melissa flushed crimson at the thinly-veiled insolence and hostility in the woman's tone. Stiffly she confronted the housekeeper.

'Why do you resent the fact that Mr Graham and I care for each other?'

The habit of rigid self-control struggled with the strong emotion that sought to break through on Mrs Edgar's face.

'Care? A lonely man has fallen for the tricks of a girl who set out to attract him. I am the one who cares for him! For eight years I have worked for him, and in all that time I doubt if he has looked at me properly once. But my happiness has come from seeing that his home was pleasant and welcoming. For eight years I have carried out my duties better than any wife could have done, but now you have come, trading on your youth and his pity, and as a result I will lose everything.'

She covered her face with her hands, unable to control her harsh sobs. Quickly she turned and hurried away, her shoulders shaking. Melissa slowly made her way to her rooms. She had fallen almost accidentally into love, and had quickly found that love returned. It took an effort to try to imagine the years Mrs Edgar had spent in constant contact with Edward Graham, knowing that he would never love her and would never even realise that she loved him. Could anything be worse?

Melissa was reluctant to encounter the housekeeper the following morning, but she found with relief that Mrs Edgar was carrying out her duties with her usual impassive dignity. Melissa felt very alone when Edward had left for London, however. Tired of the house and gardens where she felt perpetually under the observation of Mrs Edgar, Melissa took herself off for a long walk along the surrounding lawns.

Depression spoiled her enjoyment of the summer beauty. Loving Edward had seemed so easy at first, until they had realised that her unknown past might hold secrets that could threaten that love. Now she was aware that the future would put that love to the test as well. Mrs Edgar would not be the only one to think that she had deliberately set out to trap a rich man.

She remembered how Nurse Woods

had disliked him, and her own uncertain reaction to him at the hospital. What would the nurse think when she heard that they were to be wed? She had assured Carole Cardus that there was nothing between her and Edward, and that she sometimes saw Halford Manor as a comfortable prison. What would Carole think when she heard the latest news?

Her heart lifted, however, as she approached Halford Manor and saw Edward's car outside. Thank heavens he was back! No matter what other people said and felt, when she was with him their mutual love and trust in their future together seemed beyond doubt.

She was surprised to see a dashing white sports car there as well. Edward jealously guarded his privacy and usually refused to allow business associates to call on him at the manor, so who had been allowed to visit him at home? As she reached the flight of steps, the front door opened and Edward himself ushered out a slim, tanned man with a shock of white hair. This guest must have been welcome, for both men were smiling and talking easily to each other.

Melissa stood waiting as the two men came down towards the white car. Edward's face lit up as it always did when he saw her, and for a few seconds they were aware only of each other. Eagerly he came to her, an arm sliding possessively round her shoulders as he dropped a kiss on her hair.

'Doctor King, I would like you to meet Melissa.'

The white-haired man shook her hand, and she was conscious of both his firm grasp and the keen, objective survey he was making of her.

'I am delighted to have even this brief meeting with you, Melissa.'

He turned to Edward as he released her hand.

'I can understand your anxiety and impatience now, my friend. I hope all goes well, and that I will hear good news.'

Briskly he settled himself in the car, waved goodbye, and drove off rapidly down the drive. Melissa lifted an enquiring eyebrow.

'A charming man, but who is he, and why did you let him come here?'

Edward chuckled as he led her inside the house.

'Let him come? I've been begging him, entreating him to come. Let's go into the drawing-room and I'll explain.'

She settled on one of the deep couches, tucking her legs under her as Edward sat on the edge of an armchair, leaning forward eagerly.

'Dr King is a leading authority on head injuries and their after-effects. I wanted to discuss your case with him, and see whether he could do anything or give us any advice.'

Hope lit up her face.

'What did he say? Is there a chance of curing my amnesia?'

'He could hardly decide that just on the information I could give him. Datchett House sent him the notes on your case at my request, however. I asked him to stay and examine you but he said that from what he had learned there is someone else, an expert in amnesia, who would be much more likely to be able to help. Dr Streicher has a clinic in Switzerland, in Geneva. You would have to go there.'

'Switzerland? Could I go there? Would he have me as a patient?'

Her experience with Mrs Edgar had strengthened her desire to reclaim her past. Only when she was a whole woman in full possession of the facts about her life could she convince others that she was marrying Edward because she loved him and not because she saw him as a solution to her problems.

Edward was striding round the big room now, as though his eager energy had to be released somehow.

'He has agreed. That is why Dr King was here. Now we just have to arrange to take you to his clinic.'

Telephone calls to Switzerland were easy to make. Persuading various bodies to allow a woman without a passport, birth certificate or any evidence or knowledge of her identity to leave the country proved more difficult. There were many obstacles to be overcome by delicate negotiation, and it was some time before Edward could announce triumphantly that they would soon be free to travel.

'I began to think the problems would never be solved,' he admitted one evening after dinner.

A log fire was taking the first chill of autumn out of the air, and Melissa was resting secure in the comfort of Edward's arms.

'When can we leave? From which airport do we fly to Geneva?' she enquired drowsily.

'Well, actually, I thought it might be best to take the ferry across the Channel and spend a few days in Paris before driving on to Geneva,' he admitted.

She looked up at him reprovingly.

'I suppose there isn't some little

business matter that needs your personal attention in Paris, is there?'

'Honestly, my dearest, it will only take two or three hours, but it does need to be seen to. Anyway, I want to show you Paris. A couple of days won't make all that difference to your treatment.'

'I'll see Paris with you with pleasure,' she said softly.

Preparations for the journey were soon made. Edward was to go to London on business two days before Melissa was to leave Halford Manor and she was to meet him in Dover, where they would spend the night at a hotel before taking the early-morning ferry to Calais.

Those two days without him at Halford Manor dragged by very slowly. Swept along by Edward's confidence, Melissa had begun to accept it as a certainty that Dr Streicher would be able to restore her memory, and she was eager to start the journey to him. She was conscious, too, of Mrs Edgar's watchful eyes following her constantly.

With Edward Graham gone, the house-keeper's silent animosity was becoming obvious again.

It was a relief to Melissa, therefore, when the time finally came to leave. Her cases had been put in the car which waited at the foot of the steps. In the entrance hall, Mrs Edgar waited by the door for any final instructions.

'Mr Graham will let you know, of course, when he will be coming back,' Melissa said.

'I shall look forward to seeing him again,' the housekeeper said smoothly.

'I shall come back at the same time if my treatment is complete,' Melissa added.

'Of course, miss, if you do come back.'

'Why shouldn't I?' Melissa demanded challengingly.

'We don't know yet what happened in your past. That discovery may alter everything.'

Melissa picked up her handbag and left without another word to the housekeeper, but as the black limousine began its long journey to Dover she looked back at the gracious house until it was lost to sight. Of course she would return! Halford Manor was her home and would be the home she would share with Edward. If Mrs Edgar could not accept the situation then she would be the one to leave, no matter how sorry Melissa felt for her.

She told herself to forget the bitterness of a jealous woman and relaxed in the comfortable seat, but with a tiny frown persisting between her brows. Could anything in her past ruin her hopes for the future? Edward had said that perhaps she could not remember because subconsciously she wanted to blot out something in the past. Could she be avoiding the memory of something shameful, or even a crime? She lifted her chin resolutely. She would face any problems from the past when her knowledge of it had been restored and she would deal with them as they arose. Meanwhile she would not let any shadow spoil the coming days with Edward in Paris.

She found herself twisting the ring Edward had given her. It was a little too big for safety, she thought, so she slipped it off her finger and stowed it safely in an inner pocket of her handbag. The car drove on southwards as Melissa turned her thoughts to the days ahead and wondered how Dr Streicher would treat her. She felt the cold touch of fear. If the doctor failed, there would be no hope left, and she would not be able to marry Edward.

Casually glancing out of a window, she saw that the number of houses was increasing as they neared a town. Soon they were passing through quiet streets drowsing in the early autumn sun. Melissa became aware of increasing mental agitation. Some thought, some idea was trying to break through from her subconscious. She had to stop and think. Impulsively she reached out and gripped the chauffeur's shoulder.

'Could you stop?' she began, but

didn't get any further.

It was sheer misfortune that a dog should have darted out from behind a parked car just as the chauffeur was distracted by Melissa's touch. Swerving instinctively to avoid the dog, he lost control for a vital second, and there was the horrifying crunch of glass and metal as he hit a lamp post.

7

Melissa leaned against the wall, breathless with shock. A large black car had demolished a lamp-post and had come to rest at a slight angle, the passenger door hanging open. She could see a man in a chauffeur's uniform slumped over the wheel apparently unconscious. The noise of the impact had summoned people from the nearby houses.

'Are you all right, love?' one woman questioned Melissa. 'You look as white as a sheet!'

'I think it must have just caught me as it came round the corner. I feel as if I'll have some bruises tonight,' Melissa replied.

'You should get the doctor to have a look at you. I dialled emergency so the ambulance should be here soon for the driver. You could go with him.'

'No, thank you. I'm all right, really.

I'd better get back to work.'

Melissa looked round in confusion. Now why was she here? She'd probably been sent out to get some cakes for the afternoon tea-break. It was an errand that usually fell to her, after all. Oh, well, they would have to do without cakes today, but she would be grateful for a cup of tea and a quiet five minutes to get over the shock.

As the growing crowd around the car parted to make way for the ambulance, she slipped away and made her way through the familiar streets until she reached the white building which presented a blank, windowless wall to the street, with just a small brass plate reading **MacAdam: Architectural Restoration**. The main entrance to the firm was on the left where she could see a plate-glass door giving a glimpse of a receptionist at a desk but Melissa made her way round to the right of the building, to an anonymous dark green door.

She turned the handle and went in,

past the half-dozen coats and jackets hanging on a row of hooks, and slowly climbed the narrow, uncarpeted flight of stairs. At the top was a door whose frosted glass let enough light pass through to illuminate the landing while hiding what lay beyond.

The room it opened into was large, and the uncurtained windows occupied nearly all of one wall, filling the room with light. The room was equipped with drawing tables and computers. In one corner an electric kettle with a few mugs, a packet of tea-bags and a jar of instant coffee emphasised the utilitarian nature of the room.

A short man with untidy light brown hair and glasses looked up from a computer screen which he had been studying as she entered, and nodded at her abstractedly as she stood hesitantly in the doorway. Suddenly he looked up again. Amazement dawned on his face, and he stood up so abruptly that his chair fell over.

'Liss! Where have you been?'

She sank down, resting her head in her hands.

'Hello, Malcolm. I went to Crown Street, as usual, and a car crashed. It just caught me, I think. I've definitely got some sore bits.'

She lifted her head and gave him a wan smile.

'Could you be a dear and make me a cup of tea? I'll just go to the cloakroom and tidy myself up.'

As he continued to stare at her she went out the door that led out into the rest of the building. In the cloakroom she shut the door and then leaned against it with her eyes closed. She really did feel very dizzy! The car must have hit her harder than she thought. Taking a deep breath, she straightened up and opened her eyes, and found herself looking directly into the full-length mirror on the wall. Her eyes widened, and she looked at her reflection in disbelief.

She saw an elegant woman in a fashionable suit, her feathery hair framing the attractive face dominated by striking hazel eyes. The deep green leather bag she clasped matched the high-heeled shoes she wore. Melissa blinked, shook her head, and looked again. The same vision looked back at her with the bewilderment she herself was feeling.

Concussion! That was it! The car must have hit her harder than she had thought, and the reflection was a fantasy. What the mirror should have shown, as she well knew, was a rather dumpy figure in comfortable flat shoes, dressed in dull clothes chosen for their wearing qualities and ease of maintenance, clothes that never dated because they were never fashionable. If only she did look like the figure in the mirror!

The Melissa realised that she was looking down at herself, and seeing a light green skirt and dark green shoes. Desperately she fumbled for the door handle and fled back to the room where Malcolm stood waiting for her with a mug of tea. As she collapsed into a chair, he handed it to her without a word and stood by silently.

She held the mug's warmth gratefully and took a few sips of the strong brew before she looked up at him.

'What's happened to me, Malcolm?'

He pulled out the chair opposite, sat down and shrugged his shoulders.

'I was waiting for you to tell me that, Liss. You walked out of here six months ago without a word to anyone and just vanished. We haven't heard a word, neither has your landlady, and then ten minutes ago you walk back in behaving as if you'd just popped out to the shops, and looking very different!'

'But I just went to get some cakes, and then the car hit me.'

He looked at her steadily and her voice faded.

'Six months?' she said incredulously. 'What on earth have I been doing?'

'You've been doing very well, by the look of you, Liss.'

'Don't call me Liss. That's not my name.'

'It's what you've always been called.'

'No I haven't! I'm called . . .'

The vague memory fled, dispelled by the sound of the door opening. A tall, fair-haired man entered then halted abruptly, staring at her in disbelief. Delighted colour flooded her cheeks as she stood up and stretched out her arms to him.

'John!'

She ran to meet him, throwing her arms round his neck. As he hugged her she gratefully let her head rest on his chest. Whatever had happened to her, John would look after her. After all, he was the man she loved, who loved her in return. She let him lead her back to her chair where he took the seat beside her, his arm comfortingly round her shoulders. She was aware of the urgent look of appeal he gave Malcolm, who rapidly explained what had happened.

'Can you remember anything of the last few months?' John asked.

'I don't know. I'm not sure. There are so many pictures in my head, but it's all a jumble. The last thing I remember clearly is being here.'

She thought she felt his arm go tense. 'What do you remember about here?'

She tried to put her memories into some coherent order. MacAdam's was a small firm which specialised in the repair and renovation of old buildings. She had started work with them as a combination of secretary and general assistant, and had then discovered her own love of architecture. She had used her spare time to increase her knowledge and at work she'd learned from the discussions between Malcolm Byrd and John Norris in the drawing-office.

She had been rather shy of John Norris, a good-looking extrovert with a high opinion of himself, who saw himself as unofficially MacAdam's righthand man. Attractive, confident men were outside her experience and he took little notice of her until he came into the office unexpectedly one lunch-time and found her bent over a sheet of drawing paper. He peered over her shoulder.

'That looks good. Mind if I have a closer look?'

She had jumped, unaware of his presence until he spoke.

'It's just something I was trying,' she said, blushing as she reluctantly let him see what she had been drawing. 'I heard you and Malcolm talking about the fireplace you need for the house you're starting on soon, and I was sketching an idea I had for it.'

John Norris drew the sheet of paper towards him and looked at the sketch with interest. It was rough, with the lines hesitantly drawn, but the design itself was attractive and definitely suitable for the period in which that particular house had been built.

'Not bad,' he commented, picking up the sheet. 'Have you done anything else?'

Flattered, she shyly handed him a folder.

'I'm interested in architecture,' she

136

said, 'and I have tried to make a few designs of my own.'

He leafed through the half-a-dozen other sketches, and had pursed his lips in a silent whistle. Like the fireplace, they were hesitant in execution, but showed knowledge and imagination. He examined them with close attention.

'Very promising,' he had said, for the first time giving her the full benefit of his charming, blue-eyed smile. 'Would you mind if I kept this fireplace drawing? It's given me an idea.'

'Of course,' she had stammered. 'Please keep it if you feel it might help you.'

Blushing again, she told him how pleased she would be if he could make use of it. It had vanished into his pocket as Malcolm came into the room, and a few days later she was delighted to find that John Norris had presented her idea skilfully redrawn but otherwise unaltered to Mr MacAdam, who was going to use it for the house. Somehow Mr MacAdam had never learned that the design had originally come from Liss.

She didn't mind, however. The incident seemed to have made John Norris aware of her. After a few days he asked her to join him in the pub for a drink after work. She sat there nursing half a pint of lager while he did the talking, mostly about himself. She was too inexperienced to conceal her admiration of him, and he began to ask her out regularly. After all, she was quite a pretty girl really, and he enjoyed her frank adoration.

For the first time in her life, Melissa had been happy. She had found someone who seemed to care for her, and she felt wanted and loved, escaping from the shadows of her dismal childhood. As all these memories came rushing back now, she smiled happily at John.

'I remember working here with you two, and I remember us being together, John.'

She felt the tension in his arm relax.

'Is that all you remember?' Malcolm

asked, and there was an edge to his voice.

John looked at him sharply.

'Yes,' she responded. 'Why? Have I forgotten anything important?'

'No, of course not,' John said hastily. 'There's no problem about that. What we must find out is what has happened to you during the last six months before you walked back into my life.'

Malcolm pointed to the green hand-bag.

'There should be some clues there.'

She opened it almost nervously and tipped out its contents, It contained the expected comb and handkerchief, a purse with some notes in it and some expensive cosmetics, but that was all. There were no letters, no diary, no cheque book or official papers, no clues. She sank back, disappointed, suddenly aware that those few items in the bag were apparently all she possessed in the world. What about food and shelter for the night?

'It's no use,' she said despondently. 'I

think I'd better go and see my old landlady and find out what she did with the things I left.'

'I'd come with you,' John Norris said, 'but I've got to see MacAdam and do some work before I can finish here. Will you meet me at the restaurant opposite about seven?'

She nodded, disappointed a little that he wasn't prepared to drop everything to be with her, but that feeling faded as he smiled into her eyes and then dropped a light kiss on her brow.

'Don't vanish again,' her warned her.

She smiled back and promised to be at the restaurant, at the same time wondering why Malcolm was looking so cynical.

The interview with her former landlady was very depressing. Once the woman had recognised her she seemed more ready to talk about back rent and storage charges than find Melissa's property. She said it was stored in the cellar, and she certainly couldn't find it and get it out there and then, and

Melissa's room had long been let, so she couldn't stay there for the night.

Melissa was therefore at the restaurant before seven, and had time to have a drink and think quietly before John arrived. She was puzzled at the fact that although she could remember the months she had worked at MacAdam's, she could not remember leaving, nor why she had left. What had happened since, what had motivated her to abandon work, lodgings and everything she possessed?

John arrived and ordered them both drinks without asking her what she wanted and then sat looking at her with open admiration.

'Something's changed you, Liss. I always thought you were quite pretty, but now you're beautiful, glamorous.'

She smiled her thanks, then told him about the landlady and her plan to stay at a small hotel for the night. He listened with interest, but seemed more eager to know what she planned to do about MacAdam's.

141

'He'll take you back. He appreciated how good you were at your job.'

'I've got to find out what happened to me first. Anyway, I doubt if he will want to re-employ me after I've vanished for six months.'

'He will when I've talked to him about it. You can trust me.'

Suddenly it was as though there had been a small explosion in her brain. She dropped her fork and stared at him with wide eyes.

'You've said that to me before!'

He frowned at her.

'So what?'

'So,' she said slowly, 'I've just remembered why I ran away.'

The memory of the time leading up to her disappearance had returned . . .

As they both worked at MacAdam's, it had seemed natural to her that she and John should sometimes discuss work matters in their leisure time, and quite often she found that her suggestions or designs had been adopted. For a while she simply felt flattered, and it

142

was Malcolm who first made her question the situation.

'Liss,' he said tentatively one day while John was in MacAdam's office, 'I know that John has been using some ideas he got from you, because I've seen him copying your drawings. Don't you think he ought to tell MacAdam who was responsible for the ideas so that you can get the credit that's due to you? MacAdam might even move you from secretarial work to the drawing-office itself.'

When Melissa had nerved herself to mention this to John, however, he had looked furious.

'What business has Malcolm to interfere in my affairs?'

'He wasn't interfering in your affairs. He was trying to help me with mine. And I think he may have a point. Why don't you tell MacAdam about the way I've helped you?'

John regained his self-control and forced a smile.

'Don't you think I care about you and

want to help you? MacAdam has some very old-fashioned views. He doesn't think women are any good as architects. When he's accepted enough of your designs without knowing where they come from, then I'll tell him about you.'

He put his arm round her.

'Does it really matter which of us gets the credit? After all, if I'm promoted, the extra money will benefit both of us.'

He drew her close to him.

'If it's enough, then perhaps we could consider some more permanent relationship.'

'You mean we could get married?'

He smiled down at her meaningfully, too careful to actually put the promise into words.

'I know how important money is,' she admitted, 'but I still want recognition and status in return for the work I do. It's only fair!'

'Of course,' he murmured into her hair. 'I realise now that you have your own ambitions. But I've got to choose the right time. Now if you could think of a good design for this latest drawing-room fireplace that's needed, it would be extremely helpful, and perhaps I could tell him then.'

'By the end of the week I'll have the drawings ready, and they'll be good.'

'Then let's stop arguing. Let me have your design and of course I'll tell MacAdam. You're right, of course. I should have told him about you ages ago, but he's a difficult man and I was always waiting for just the right time. This time I will. You can trust me.'

He took her in his arms and she relaxed against him, telling herself that she had been stupid to suspect him of just using her. How could a girl who knew so little about men understand him?

So she drew up plans for the fireplace, John Norris collected them, and also took all her rough work, saying that he might want to use different elements of the plans. He redrew them and presented them to his boss.

Now, as she sat at the restaurant table, Melissa was remembering that bitter morning when MacAdam had made one of his rare visits to the drawing-office. He had bustled in and gone straight to John, shaking him warmly by the hand.

'Congratulations, John! I've just seen your drawings. That fireplace is the centrepiece of the room and it needed to be something outstanding. You've given me just what was needed. This follows a lot of other good work recently. There'll be a new contract for you soon.'

Melissa was standing quietly ready by a table. This was the big moment. This would be when John would turn to her and introduce her to MacAdam as the real creator of the design. Instead, he had accepted the congratulations and ignored her. It was only when MacAdam had left the room, followed by Malcolm, that he turned defiantly to meet her accusing gaze.

'You didn't tell him it was my work.

Why not? You promised you would!' she exclaimed.

'Does it matter? As I said, if you really loved me you'd be glad to help me get promotion instead of wanting a lot of fuss made over you.'

She felt close to tears.

'I'm not just your girl friend, John. I'm a person in my own right, and I want recognition for what I do.'

'Well, it's too late this time.'

She faced him defiantly and shook her head.

'No, it isn't. I can go to Mr MacAdam and tell him the truth.'

He took an angry step towards her, and she flinched at his threatening expression.

'Do you mean you'd make me look a fool?'

'I mean that I'd tell him you are a thief who has stolen my ideas.'

Suddenly he relaxed, laughing at her.

'And how are you going to prove that?'

'I can show him my drawings.'

'Which no longer exist. I took them all, remember?'

She gasped, then thought rapidly.

'Malcolm will support me. He knows you've used my work.'

'Malcolm? Everybody knows he's jealous of me and would say anything to hurt me. So who's MacAdam going to believe — his right-hand man or a dull little secretary who's being spiteful because she's got a crush on me but I don't fancy her? He's going to ask you why you never said anything before.'

Her dream of achievement and her dream of love were collapsing together.

'I'll never help you any more. What will you say when you can't produce such good work again?' she demanded.

He grinned at her.

'By then I'll have my new contract. All I have to do now is tell him that I'm finding it difficult to concentrate because you keep pestering me, and you'll be out of a job, Miss Smith!'

Tears blurred her vision as she stumbled out of the room, leaving him to enjoy his shabby triumph. She could never work at MacAdam's again. She had to get away. She went straight back to her lodgings and packed a small case, then headed for the railway station. She bought a ticket to London with no clear idea of what she would do when she got there.

When she had sunk down in her seat on the London train, however, the full misery of her position had struck her. She had lost everything — her job and the man she thought had loved her. Tears began to creep down her cheeks, and she wiped them away with her handkerchief. She was aware that a woman opposite was looking at her suspiciously. Melissa felt that she couldn't face either pity or contempt, and when the train had stopped at a small station she had seized her bag and got off.

The station had been a short distance outside a small town and she had started to walk to it along the country roads. Absorbed in her misery, she hadn't heard the car's approach until its headlights lit up the road . . .

8

Back in the present now, her rediscovered past still vivid in her memory, Melissa realised that John Norris was staring at her, waiting for her to speak. When she stayed silent he stretched out his hand to seize hers.

'Liss, you don't know how glad I am to see you!'

She looked at him with surprise. Why was he so pleased to see her after the way they had parted? What had happened to him? He hurried on, as if he wanted to imprint his version of events on her memory before her own recollection became too clear.

'I don't know if you remember everything now, but the day you vanished we'd had a stupid disagreement. I looked for you to try to make it up, but there's been no sign of you all this time. I've been desperately worried.

After all, we meant so much to each other, I couldn't believe you'd leave me without a word.'

She looked at this man she'd adored, seeing him with fresh eyes after their separation. Could she really have broken her heart over him? She realised that the charm that had dazzled her was superficial. None of these thoughts showed as she smiled at him and gently withdrew her hand from his grasp.

'Did we quarrel? I'm afraid some things are still a bit vague,' she answered.

She glimpsed relief in his eyes. Melissa was surprised to find that she felt no bitterness or anger towards him. Her involvement with him had just been a step on the way to her growing maturity, and she wondered only how she could have let herself be deceived by him. She realised that disillusionment had begun to set in even before their final confrontation.

She should have stayed and fought him. With Malcolm's support and the evidence of earlier work she could have exposed him. It had been the pressure of personal feeling as well as work that had made an inexperienced girl break and run. She stood up, smoothing her skirt with hands that trembled a little.

'And now I'd better go and try to book a room for the night.'

'But we've got to talk!'

'Have we anything to say to each other?' she enquired coolly.

His head jerked up in amazement.

'Liss! We loved each other!'

'I thought it was my work you loved,' she commented, the old bitterness emerging briefly.

He had the grace to blush before hurrying to reassure her.

'I told you that was a silly misunderstanding, Liss. I was in an awkward situation. You should have given me time to think.'

So it had all been her fault! Now his tone became quieter, more intimate, as he leaned over the table toward her.

'I can't tell you how much I've missed

you. You can't just vanish again. I want you back desperately.'

There were beads of perspiration on his forehead, and there was real urgency and desperation in his voice, but Melissa could not believe that it was because he loved her. She sat down again, pushing her chair back a little to distance herself from him.

'You want me back all right,' she mused. 'But what's the real reason? And before you start, I might as well tell you that I now remember everything that happened between us, so don't try to lie to me.'

He tried to look indignant, but there was a shifty look about his eyes, and as she waited silently for his reply his pretence of love collapsed together with his pride.

'It's MacAdam,' he groaned. 'He can't understand why I'm not producing such good work nowadays. He's obviously suspicious about the reason, and he's been hinting that if I can't start producing high-level designs again, I'd better start looking for another job.'

Idly Melissa played with a fork, wondering how she could ever have cared for such a fool.

'So you want me back?'

'Yes!'

'So that I can go on turning out designs which you'll say are your work.'

'We'll work together, Liss. It will help both of us. We'll get married, then it won't matter who gets the credit.'

'I told you I'd remembered everything. I've heard all this before.'

He heard the boredom in her voice, but could not believe that the old charm would not work.

'Liss, my darling . . . '

He looked at her unresponsive face, and his voice grew higher, so that some of the other diners turned to look at them.

'Come back to me, Liss. I love you!'

She was aware of the people staring from other tables. All she felt was embarrassment, the urge to escape from this desperate, foolish man and never see him again, but before she could free her hand and rise she heard another voice.

'A little melodramatic for such a public place, but very touching. I'm sure the lady will soon be persuaded.'

Melissa looked up in surprise, and saw a tall man with high cheek bones looking down at them with cold grey eyes. She wondered why a total stranger should interrupt their quarrel. Or did she know him? Had he worked at MacAdam's? There was something vaguely familiar about him.

He loomed over their table, while John Norris gaped up at him in surprise.

'I'm afraid I've appeared earlier than you expected,' the stranger said icily to Melissa. 'When the chauffeur telephoned me from the hospital and told me what had happened I dropped everything and came in search of you. I thought you might need help. By luck, I saw you come in here.'

He nodded contemptuously at John Norris.

'I didn't realise that you already had an eager companion. So this is the man you really love?'

'What concern is it of yours?' she asked, but he didn't seem to hear her.

'Tell me,' he continued, 'did you ever really lose your memory? Were you afraid that Dr Streicher would expose you for a fake, or was it that you couldn't stay away from your lover any longer and had to see him before you went to Switzerland?'

His words didn't make sense to her, but before she could reply, John Norris, as bewildered as Melissa but anxious to impress her, had stumbled awkwardly to his feet.

'Stop talking to Liss like that!'

The stranger rounded on him.

'I shall talk to her how I like. I have earned the right. In fact I've paid handsomely for it.'

The sneering tone was enough to provoke John Norris, on edge already, and he swung a wild fist at the intruder who took the blow easily on his forearm. Before a fight could develop further, two waiters, already alerted by the raised voices, had closed in on the pair.

Under cover of the confusion, Melissa seized her handbag, fled from the scene, and raced along the road toward the railway station. Panting, she reached the ticket office just as the noise of a train approaching could be heard.

'Where's that train going?' she demanded.

'It's the London express.'

'Then give me a ticket, please!'

She handed over some notes and grabbed the change, hurrying to the platform just in time to board the train and sink down in an empty corner seat. She gazed out of the window as the train gathered pace, half-expecting to see John Norris or the stranger appear on the platform in pursuit of her, but it was empty, and she sank with a sigh of relief as the train sped on.

Once again she was running away, but

this time it was anger and not a broken heart that drove her. John Norris had dared hope that she would go back to him, just to save his stupid career! And she didn't know who the stranger had been in the restaurant, but it had been clear that he was far from friendly. If he was a figure from the missing six months she never wanted to see him again either!

Something drastic had happened to her during that time, however. She was aware that her thoughts and behaviour were very different from the Liss Smith who had worked at MacAdam's and fallen for John Norris.

She had been christened Melissa, after the grandmother whose brooch she had inherited, but all her life she had been called Liss. Her mother had been widowed when Melissa was a baby and the girl had grown up in a world where money was always short, with a mother whose nature had been soured by the constant struggle to cope.

Melissa had left school as soon as it

was possible so that she could start earning money in a series of secretarial jobs. There was no cash to spare for a social life, so she had found relief from dull work and her mother's constant complaints in an interest in the arts, particularly architecture. It cost nothing to observe the style and detail of buildings.

When her mother had died unexpectedly, Melissa had been twenty and desperate for a change. She had applied for a post as general assistant at MacAdam's, and there she had met John Norris. Looking back, she could forgive that inexperienced Melissa for thinking she was in love with the first man who showed any interest in her. But whatever happened in the future, she would be in control.

With this firm resolve, she drifted into a doze until the train reached London. Once there, however, practical matters took over. With the advice of one of the transport police, she found a room for the night in a cheap but respectable hotel. As she paid, she was taken aback to see how little money was left in her purse. In her room she carefully hung up her suit and blouse and rinsed her underwear in the wash-basin. Having taken care of her clothes, it was time to see what else she had in the world.

Her purse now held just over two pounds! She scrabbled through the comb and cosmetics to see if any loose coins had fallen to the bottom of the bag, but was disappointed. Then her probing fingers felt a lump in the lining, and she realised that she had overlooked the interior pocket.

She opened it, felt inside, and found she was grasping a ring whose stones flashed with such dazzling fire she was almost sure that they were diamonds. She tried it on, turning her hand to admire the way it caught the light. Was it hers? Had she stolen it? There was no way of knowing, and she took it off and put it back in the pocket, which contained nothing else but a small rectangle of white card.

Gordon and Carole Cardus, it read, and there was a London address and telephone number. Melissa considered the card. It didn't look like a business card, and she must have kept it for a purpose. Could they be friends? Well, she decided, with two pounds in her purse and no-one to turn to, she would have to find out. The ring could stay where it was until she knew more about its ownership.

This decided, she climbed into bed feeling surprisingly calm. Her life lay empty before her. She had a bed for the night and two pounds. Beyond that, she had the clothes she had been wearing that day. But she had been alone or lonely for most of her life and she had coped. She could do so again, and this time she would have the benefit of the lessons she had learned from her experiences with John Norris.

She slept well.

It was early the next morning when Melissa slipped quietly out of the hotel. The streets were full of commuters.

When she had found a telephone box free she took out the small white card and arranged her few remaining coins in front of her and then dialled the number on the card with hesitant fingers. She heard the telephone ring four, five, six times, and then the receiver was lifted.

'Hello?' a sleepy female voice said, obviously not best pleased to be disturbed.

'Carole?' Melissa ventured.

'Yes. Who's there?'

Who indeed? Melissa hesitated, and her free hand went to the gold brooch at the neck of her blouse.

'Melissa,' she almost whispered.

The voice at the end of the line suddenly became wide awake.

'Melissa? Where are you? What's the matter?'

She couldn't speak. Just as a phrase spoken by John Norris had triggered her memory, so the sound of the woman's voice combined with the touch of the brooch seemed to have lifted the curtain which hid the mystery of those six missing months. She suddenly remembered the hospital, then Halford Manor, Edward . . .

She remembered the great car and the sound as it hit the lamp post, and she realised the full significance of the scene in the restaurant with the stranger! He had been Edward!

'Melissa!'

There was a note of urgency in Carole's voice.

'Carole, I'm in London and I need help,' Melissa whispered.

'Where are you?'

She looked round. She could see a small café nearby and gave Carole its name and location, and was told to wait there. Melissa put the receiver down, went into the café and ordered a cup of coffee. Waiting for Carole gave her a chance to assemble her thoughts about the previous evening.

Edward had obviously rushed to help her, but as soon as he had seen her with John Norris he had assumed that she had been deceiving him and didn't give her a chance to explain, either about John or the fact that at that moment she hadn't even recognised Edward. Theirs had seemed a perfect love, but with a few angry words he had shown how shallow it was.

She sipped the coffee very slowly, her eyes on the door. Even so, the cup had been empty for some time, and the proprietor was giving her meaningful looks before the door finally opened and the figure she had been expecting appeared. Carole Cardus sank down opposite her and imperiously beckoned the owner, ordering fresh coffee for both women.

'Do you know,' she said in tones of horror, 'that I had to wait five minutes for a taxi? I don't think I've ever been out so early in my life!'

Then she looked at Melissa properly, and her eyes narrowed.

'What on earth's the matter? You look as if something dreadful has happened. I'll never forgive Edward Graham if he's hurt you! Tell me all about it.'

As briefly as she could, Melissa gave her a summary of what had happened and what she had remembered in the last twenty-four hours. The other woman listened attentively and gave her a look of real sympathy when she had finished.

'You poor thing! You have got bad taste in men, haven't you? Norris sounds horrible, and trust Edward Graham to assume that you were taking advantage of him. Now, what do you want me to do? Shall I call Edward and tell him what you've told me? It may take some time to find him.'

'No!' Melissa said passionately. 'I've been thinking about what he said. I can see why he jumped to the wrong conclusions but if he really loved me he should have trusted me instead of assuming I'd been deceiving him. If you tell him my side of the affair it will seem as if I'm begging him to take me back, and I'm not going to. I'm going to start a new life, free of John Norris and free of Edward Graham.'

Carole held up a warning hand.

'That sounds very fine, but don't be in too much of a hurry. Edward has probably come to his senses by now, and you don't throw away life with a millionaire in a fit of temper.'

Melissa remembered the humiliating scene in the restaurant, the accusations Edward had flung at her.

'I wouldn't go back to Edward if he begged me to!'

'Yes, that sounds very well, but what are you going to do instead?'

'Work,' Melissa said simply.

'Work?' Carole blinked at the idea. 'At what?'

'I'm a perfectly competent secretary and they're always in demand,' Melissa returned. 'All I need is somewhere to sleep and a chance to look through advertisements and contact some agencies. I've decided to go to Manchester. It's a big city, so I should find it easy to get work, and I don't think Edward Graham has any connections there.'

'But Manchester's a long way away,'

Carole observed. 'Suppose you need more help? You'd better keep in touch with me.'

'Of course I will,' Melissa told her, 'on condition you promise that you'll never help Edward find me.'

'Of course I won't!' Carole said warmly, but Melissa thought she had glimpsed an evasive flicker in her eyes.

'Thank you. The other thing is, I've hardly any money.'

'No problem. I'll write you a cheque.'

Melissa shook her head.

'At the moment I doubt if I can cash it.'

Rapidly Carole looked through her bag.

'I've got some money. You can have that.'

A handful of notes was pushed discreetly across the table and Melissa took them gratefully.

'I'll pay you back as soon as I can.'

'Don't be silly. Take it, and the best of luck.'

Melissa tucked the money in her bag

and looked up to see Carole checking the time anxiously.

'Have you got to go?'

'I've got an appointment at my hairdresser's. Remember him? Ring me this afternoon and we'll meet again. It will give me a chance to get some more cash as well.'

They parted outside the café. Carole hailed a taxi and quickly embraced Melissa in a cloud of expensive perfume.

'Remember, call me later,' were her last words out of the taxi window.

Melissa nodded vigorously. But although Carole's intentions might be good now, Melissa was not sure that her friend would be able to resist the opportunity to get in Edward's good books if he indicated that he wanted information about Melissa. Once she had seen Carole out of sight, therefore, Melissa went to catch a train to Bath, on the simple grounds that it was a long way from Manchester!

In Bath, tourist information helped

her find a small bed-and-breakfast hotel where she paid for a week in advance, using up a large chunk of her cash to do so. She also had to buy some tights and underwear and a few toiletries. Once again, her money was running dangerously low. Obviously finding a job would be a priority!

The next morning, with the help of a local paper and the telephone directory she began to look for work, contacting half-a-dozen firms and agencies, but difficulties arose. People were enthusiastic when they heard of her qualifications, but then they began to ask about recent experience. Her story of a long illness to cover the last few months caused their enthusiasm to fade. She didn't want to give MacAdam's for a reference because it might be used as a way of tracing her. Enthusiasm turned to politeness, and virtual offers of work had turned into, 'We'll let you know.'

By late afternoon, Melissa was tired, dispirited and depressed. Returning to her cramped room in the hotel, she considered her situation. More money was the first priority to see her through a longer job search than she had expected. There was only one possible source.

She took Edward's ring out of its hiding place. It lay in her hand, the diamonds glittering icily. Tempted, she slipped it on her ring finger and studied its beauty wistfully. Edward, she recalled, had said that it signified their love for each other. Well, the love had gone. The value of the ring would mean nothing to him, and she must forget the memories its sight brought back.

As Melissa checked her appearance before going out the following morning, she saw how her once-smart suit was beginning to look a little tired from constant wearing. She was still amazed, however, by the difference in physical appearance between the Liss Smith who worked at MacAdam's and the Melissa Smith at present staying in Bath.

Obviously part of the change was due to the loss of weight in the hospital.

Clothes bought to flatter rather than just to last were also an important factor. But there was something else. Her loss of memory had enabled her to shake off the trauma of her drab childhood, the belief implanted by her mother that she had been a burden who had spoiled her mother's chances in life. For six months she made friends with women such as Nurse Woods and Carole Cardus, and had been loved by Edward Graham. Now she had much more confidence in herself.

With the ring safely wrapped up in a tissue in her handbag, she wandered round the centre of Bath and finally went into a jeweller's shop in a side street which had a discreet notice saying that jewellery was bought as well as sold there.

'Can I help you?' the elderly man enquired from behind the polished mahogany counter.

'I have a ring I wish to sell.'

She took the ring from her bag, unwrapped it, and placed it on the counter. The man looked down at it a little disdainfully.

'Very pretty,' he commented.

'And very valuable,' she said with emphasis. 'The stones are real.'

He looked at her doubtfully, picked up the ring and examined it carefully through a lens. There was a change in his manner. The hint of patronage was gone and there was even a trace of excitement.

'I think you'd better come through to the back room,' he suggested.

With Melissa and the jeweller on each side of a small table, his approach was brisk and business-like.

'If these diamonds are as good as I think, this is a very valuable ring. Would you mind telling me how you come to have it?'

'It is mine. It was given to me as an engagement ring. The engagement has been broken off.'

'Can you tell me any more? Do you know where it was bought? Who bought it?'

'I believe it was bought in Amsterdam, but I'm not prepared to tell you by whom.'

The jeweller drummed his fingers on the table, looking from Melissa to the ring, obviously undecided.

'Look,' Melissa said in exasperation, 'I need money quickly. I know you can check the police lists to see if such a ring has been reported stolen. Either make me an offer or I'll take it somewhere else.'

He fingered the ring, clearly reluctant to let it go.

'Of course I will check those lists. If everything seems to be all right, I'll make you an offer.'

Ten minutes later, he offered her three hundred pounds.

'It's worth far more than that!' she exclaimed.

'Possibly,' the jeweller said with meaning, 'but without provenance, a knowledge of who has owned it . . . well . . . and you did say you needed money quickly.'

'Three hundred and fifty?'

He nodded agreement instantly, and she realised ruefully that she could probably have got much more but there was no time to shop around.

'I want the money in cash,' she said firmly.

He raised an eyebrow at that, but reluctantly agreed that he could give her cash. As he picked up the ring she held out her hand.

'May I hold it one last time?' she requested.

She took it from his hand and touched the large central diamond with one finger.

'This really is goodbye,' she whispered.

Her last tie with Edward was gone. Then she handed it back to the jeweller.

'Just lumps of carbon, really,' she told him, recalling something Edward had once said.

The money kept her going until she got a job with a small builder who was grateful that anyone was prepared to tackle the mountain of neglected paperwork that threatened to over-whelm his business. She found a quiet bed-sit, and settled into a placid routine. When she was not working she enjoyed the beauty of the city and also read a lot.

Most of the days were busy and she felt content. At night, however, she would sometimes lie awake thinking of the past. She had been very badly hurt by Edward's failure to trust her, and sometimes she questioned her own feelings. Had she been deceived by the aura of wealth and power and not realised what he was really like? But Melissa was sure that in those few weeks together she had come to know the real man.

She recalled what he had said about his wife and the women who had followed. When so many women had failed him, how could he know that she was different? Perhaps his reaction to the sight of her with John could be understood, if not forgiven.

At times she woke, thinking she was in his arms, and then cried herself to sleep again. What was the use of thinking about it? He had gone and they would never meet again. It would be better to forget about him and concentrate on her new life.

Melissa knew that Bath was just a respite in her life, and she knew that eventually she would want to move on to a new challenge. When spring came, she grew restless, but before she had decided on any course of action, there was a knock on her room door one Sunday morning. She opened it to find Edward Graham standing outside!

She caught her breath and froze momentarily. Then with a conscious effort she stepped back and faced him. At first he looked unchanged, but in the clear light from the uncurtained window on the landing she saw that his face looked thinner, the lines by his mouth deeper.

'How did you know I was here?' she whispered.

He held out a small jeweller's box and opened it. The diamond ring which he had given her and which she had sold glittered in the sunshine.

'The world of diamond dealing is pretty small. An Amsterdam dealer recognised this when it was offered for sale in London and informed me. I found that it had been sold in Bath and I hired an enquiry agent to find you. They telephoned me yesterday.'

She looked at him and shrugged wearily.

'I apologise. I should have sent it back to you somehow, but there was an emergency and I needed the money and you didn't.'

'You know I don't care about the money!' he burst out in a sudden fury. 'I gave you the ring and you could do what you liked with it.'

There was a discreet cough and they realised that the landlady was standing at the top of the stairs observing the scene. Edward Graham cursed under his breath, thrusting the ring back into

178

his pocket, then looked at Melissa impatiently.

'We have to talk. Where can we go?'

She took her coat down from behind the door and shrugged it on.

'There's a park five minutes' walk away.'

The short walk passed in silence. They finally came to a halt by a small lake where they sat on a bench and turned to face each other. They had been lovers, Melissa thought, but now they were as wary as enemies.

Edward looked out of place among the casually-dressed walkers in the park. He was dressed in one of his usual immaculate suits. She thought he looked more prepared for a business meeting than a personal encounter with a former love, and his opening was very brisk and business-like.

'I'm here for two reasons, Melissa. First, I owe you an apology. Seeing you with another man, apparently so close to him, was such a shock that I jumped to the wrong conclusions. I should have had more faith in you. I got the truth out of John Norris eventually. I'm sorry, Melissa. I let you down when you needed me.'

Melissa thought of all the reproaches she had wanted to hurl at him. They seemed pointless now. She realised what an effort it must have taken such a proud man to make the apology, but while his face showed regret for his actions there was no warmth, no real feeling.

'I accept your apology,' she said stiffly, 'though it's too late to make any difference now. What was the second reason?'

'I thought that perhaps you had sold the ring not just to get rid of the memory of me but because you needed the money. I had an obligation to help you if you needed it.'

A very faint hope that Melissa hadn't realised even existed died then. He was here out of a sense of duty, to make amends! Then his conscience would be satisfied and he could forget her. Well, she didn't need his charity.

'I don't want your help, thank you. Just because I was an invalid when you first met me you seem to think that I can't look after myself. In a way, I'm glad that you misjudged me and drove me away. I've got my own life now, and I don't need a white knight arriving to rescue me from any dragons!'

His lips pressed tightly together for an instant, as if he were biting back an equally hot reply.

'I see,' he said at last. 'Well, it is clear that we have no more to say to each other.'

'Goodbye!'

She flung the word at him and began to walk away rapidly before he could see the tears in her eyes.

'Melissa! Come back! I need you!'

She halted abruptly and swung round as she heard him cry out, and he strode up to her. The cold control was gone, his face and voice frankly pleading.

'You may not want me, but I need you desperately. Ever since you left nothing else has mattered. I feel as if I'm just sleep-walking through life. I shut up Halford Manor because your memory haunted it. Every time I entered a room I half-expected to see you.'

He looked down, as if ashamed of showing so much feeling.

'When the ring helped me find where you were, I dropped everything to come here. All I've got is my money, and I thought at least I could help you with that if necessary. But that was only an excuse to see you. I want you back because I love you!'

The protective wall of pride was gone. She owed him equal honesty.

'Edward, look at me.'

She stood there in a casual shirt and top worn under a cheap jacket. Her face was bare of make-up, her hair blown by the spring breeze.

'You don't know me. You are in love with Melissa, the mysterious stranger. I'm not some beautiful woman drifting from one tragic affair to another. I'm an ordinary girl in the ordinary world, earning my living and making friends. Those few months at Halford Manor with you, living in that life-style, were a time out of my life, a dream-time. There's nothing special about me. Forget me.'

She turned to go, almost unable to find the strength to turn her back on him. Blinded by tears, she did not see the dog happily dragging a small boy along and tripped over the lead that joined them. Edward leaped to catch her before she fell, seizing her in his arms. She should have pushed him away. Instead, when he bent his head to kiss her, she kissed him in return. It seemed the natural thing to do.

Finally she drew away from him, shaking her head.

'That doesn't change anything. We're still too far apart.'

He smiled down at her.

'I think we should discuss that further. It appears that you are also mistaken. You think of me as someone special, set apart by wealth and power. Well, haven't I proved by the way I treated you that I can be as big a fool as anyone? I'm an ordinary man who needs the woman he loves, someone with commonsense to remind me what life is really about. As for the way you look, don't you think I learned from Leonie that physical perfection doesn't always make a woman lovable? To me you are very beautiful.'

She looked at him uncertainly.

'I'd convinced myself that I didn't love you any more.'

'Melissa, let's have no more misunderstandings. I love you, and to me you're very special indeed. And when we kissed I could tell that you still feel for me. I need you, and I want to marry you as soon as possible.'

He took out the ring.

'I said this was the symbol of our love, and then I nearly destroyed that love. Either you wear it again or I throw it into the lake.'

He lifted his arm and prepared to

throw. Slowly she held out her left hand but then, just as he was about to take it, she snatched it back. It would be easy to give in, but she mustn't.

'No!' she exclaimed. 'I love you, and I always will, but I won't marry you. I told you that Halford Manor was like living in a dream. If I married you, I would be very happy, for a time. But I remember what it was like at Halford Manor during the days you were away, trying to think what to do.

'I couldn't endure that life for long. I would get bored and fretful and then you might wonder whether you'd made yet another mistake. Working here, in control of my own life, I'm content. I'm going to be very unhappy for a time when you go, and I'm sorry for the unhappiness that I know it will cause you, but I can't marry you and live as we did then.'

'I don't want a beautiful toy. I want a woman. If you want to study or build a career, fine. So long as your plans include our children.'

She was being offered marriage on her own terms to the man she loved!

'If you will accept a wife who won't always be waiting when you come back, and who'll be wearing jeans half the time. But I will let Carole Cardus choose my wedding dress. She'll make sure I'm a beautiful bride.'

Wordlessly he took her left hand and slid the ring on to her finger. Then Edward Graham, the rich and powerful man who prided himself on keeping apart from the rest of the world, took the woman he loved in his arms and kissed her in the middle of a public park.

When he finally let Melissa go, he looked around.

'I'm afraid this is not a very romantic place for our reunion, Melissa.'

She took his head in her hands and drew it gently down for her kiss.

'I once looked up romance in the dictionary. It said it meant fantasy, something outside ordinary life. I'll take love.'